Folly

E.L. Murray

This book is dedicated to Dr. Michael Lyles, who disproves all the themes of *Folly* by enabling me to write it in the first place.

CHAPTER 1

Norman never brought much with him, when he came to visit Servway's Protective Facility for the Criminally Insane. Only two pencils, and a scheduler in a binder that had a plastic tab labelled "notes," behind which he could keep assorted loose-leaf paper.

The notes were so he could remember details from the conversations he had with patients. Writing specifics down helped keep track of contradictory or irrational claims. Norman always tried to follow the rationale behind conversations, because it wasn't his job to point out discrepancies. He was only there to provide a friendly audience for patients who might otherwise have no chance for a normal connection with the outside world.

The binder was also useful in case anyone wanted to make a follow up appointment. He could make a note in his schedule right then and there, to make sure retirement's routine didn't zap his once sharp mind into forgetting.

He'd been coming to Servways for five years now, every Saturday and Tuesday, whenever someone wanted to talk to a visitor volunteer and specifically asked for him.

Servway's housed both criminals deemed not guilty by reason of insanity and particularly violent patients the average psychiatric hospital wasn't equipped to handle.

For confidentiality's sake, Norman was never told what these high-security criminals had done to merit incarceration. But he'd been a policeman for 21 years of his life, and before that, an apprenticed officer. He'd seen enough on the job to know both what these men were capable of, and how they suffered from the tortures of their own psyches. He'd easily passed the qualifying entry assessments that assured he'd be a good fit for volunteering.

He drove a Renault Megane up to the single row of parking spaces beside the Servway Protective Facility's double-gated entryway, parked, unclicked his seatbelt, grabbed his binder, opened the car door, closed it with a beeping click of his keys, and walked to the first set of bullet proof glass doors that slid open when he proffered a volunteer badge from an extendable lanyard's reel, clipped to his side-pocket.

He turned to peer down the double-layered chain-link fence that encircled Servway's high, cement walls. The clattering chatter of a reporter's brigade announced he wasn't the afternoon's only visitor. Hugh Cossimer, the famed actor turned philanthropist, could be seen waving a hand to one side of his head to side-step encroaching cameras.

Cossimer often came to cheer the lives of patients who were fans of his films, though, Norman had heard, the waiting list to request Cossimer as a visitor was awfully long.

"No, no, please—not today," Norman could hear Cossimer on the other side of the glass door he'd just passed through.

"Can we just ask who you'll be visiting?"

"You seem to be under the impression everyone at Servways is an infamous serial killer—"

"Have you ever been in an interview with a serial killer?"

Norman tapped his identity card and let himself in.

"Hey-ya Norm," Fred Bently was the guard between the gates today. "Got some excitement, eh?"

"Oh yeah," Fred was already stepping out from behind his desk to go tell the reporters they didn't have security clearance for further admittance.

Hugh Cossimer crowded against the glass outer doors just as Norman slipped through the inner steel turn-styles of the gated entryway's second precautionary division.

Inside, all was silent. Not even birds, really. Just level, red brick walkways. Norm followed one of these paths past a poplar tree and into the cold recesses of the clinic's outer waiting rooms, to sign his name on a waiting form at the plexi-glass opening to a protected attendant's station.

"Did he get any mail today?"

The attendant who had taken Norman's signature for processing could see he was signed in to visit Rene Cartesius. Rene was relatively new to this psych ward; he'd only been held under high security protocols for three weeks now, but he'd already asked to meet with Norman eight times. He liked Norman. He'd pointed to his name at random, at first. But he'd found in the aging pensioner someone who'd listen.

And he was always claiming the extraordinarily influential family of which he was bastard offspring would eventually send him a letter; they kept up correspondence with his mother.

"No, no mail today, sorry," the attendant turned from checking Rene's pigeon-hole.

That wasn't too unusual; patients seldom got mail, which was a blessing to the staff, who had to sort each and every envelope, to make sure no dangerous contraband snuck through. But Rene was so insistent: he'd get a letter soon; he was so sure of it.

"Has he gotten any since I was here last?"

"Nah, no chance I'm afraid,"

"Ah, too bad,"

"He's got that upcoming hearing, though,"

"Oh, really?"

"This afternoon,"

"Oh good," if the hearing went well, Rene might be able to return to a residential psychiatric facility like the one from which he had been transferred. The residential psychiatric facilities, being, as they were, unrelated to the country's prison systems, imposed fewer security measures on patients, allowed greater freedoms. "Thanks, Wade."

Norman knew practically all Servway's staff and patients by name by now. Knowing even what small insights Wade could provide gave Norman some indication of what his conversation with Rene would analyze today.

"It'll just be a few minutes," Wade left to go get the volunteers' visiting room ready.

Norman went back to sit in the fabricated-foam guest chair beside a water cooler, listening to the far-off sound of a collection of keys being turned in the lock to the hall that led to the room in which he'd shortly be visiting Rene.

Norman had come to understand the prison's system of locks and keys fairly well, though he was only ever allowed rare glimpses beyond the outer waiting and conference rooms.

From what he had seen and heard, the patients' rooms lined a hallway demarcated at either end by two doors which were both locked after 9pm, when those in residence were shepherded to bed after which the doors to their bedrooms were locked as well, to keep patients from harming one another.

Only men came to this security unit. A sister unit housed women, two towns over. Norman volunteered there sometimes too, but he found his services more often requested at Servway's facilities for men, in part simply because inmate population here was greater.

After 9am, once everyone had been woken to wash and congregate for breakfast, the doors to the hallway that led to the mens' rooms would be locked again, and the patients shepherded from the breakfast room to the communal sitting rooms to be kept under a strict ratio of six patients to every care giver.

Keeping patients from returning to their individual bedrooms enforced socializing, but it also kept them from stealing others' personal affects, an unlocked cabinet of which stood by each bolted down bed. A locked cabinet stood below this, to house the personal affects patients sometimes arrived with that might be temporarily deemed a hazard. Shoelaces, for example, were simply removed from the premises entirely, while orderlies oversaw the day to day locking of all these doors and drawers, ensuring safety by remaining dotted throughout the hallways.

"He's ready now," Wade came to collect Norman.

"Oh, perfect, thank you."

Norman was led down a hallway that flanked the communal sitting rooms, waving through an opening in the corridor to some of his other usual conversation partners. He seemed to be the only volunteer visiting this unit today.

Hugh Cossimer must have gone to some other part of the building.

"Rene's very excited today about the hearing later on," another orderly accompanying Norman prompted, swiping a final crumpled drinking cup from the meeting room's solo table.

"I heard!" Norman was genuinely excited for Rene. They all were.

He'd shown a great deal of improvement in the state of his mental health over the course of the three weeks Norman had been visiting him.

Three weeks was the minimum amount of time a patient was required to stay in higher security units like Servways, before his case could be reviewed and a panel of doctors decided whether he could be released to a less strenuously policed environment for a six-month evaluation period.

Rene seemed to be a good kid. He seemed like he could actually be out of here fairly quickly.

"Alright, Rene," An orderly led him in.

"Rene," Norman rose, hand outstretched, smiling, glad to shake hands. Both sat. The door closed. Orderlies here were very careful; they wouldn't even call patients by nicknames that weren't specifically requested by the patients themselves. This place was meant to heal, not punish.

Rene still had pinkish scarring along his left eye from the fight that had landed him in Servway's Unit for Dangerous Persons to begin with.

Unlike most of the other inmates, he hadn't come from the prison system, and he'd never been officially charged with a crime. The violent behavior for which he'd been transferred to Servways had occurred during a routine squabble at his old psychiatric ward.

"Look—look, come here; I've got to tell you something," Rene leaned forward over the table, anxious. Norman leaned forward too. "The ticket came again,"

"The ticket?"

"Yeah, the ticket from last time remember? The ticket they said I didn't have! It came again!"

Rene had started the fight that broke another inmate's ribs because others had refused to believe he'd been mailed a luggage ticket from his uncle.

"The luggage ticket?"

"The luggage ticket! It came, again! I have it in my locker right now,"

"It's the same—?"

"Same locker number 264, I knew it I knew he'd come for me, I always said he'd send me mail didn't I always say he'd send me mail?"

"Rene—? The orderlies say you haven't received any mail all this week,"

"No but that's the thing I told you my uncle's powerful enough he doesn't need to go through mail sorting he can just send it to me directly; he pulls strings, he owns this place,"

"He owns Servway? I—did you tell me that already?" Norman always explained to each patient how, as he was getting up in years, he'd have to take notes when they spoke to make sure he remembered what they said. He flipped back through his binder's notes now. There it was: 'Rene's uncle is head of Servways.'

"Oh, that's right no wait here we go I remember now—on your mother's side?"

"Well, my mother's the one who got me in this mess in the first place, 'cause, you know, she slept with my aunt's husband's brother; now he's my dad—but his brother is my uncle; he's very influential,"

Norman wrote down 'aunt's husband's brother's brother,' and then realized he may have missed a crucial step in following the family tree.

"But no incest,"

"No no, no incest," Rene was always very particular about ensuring there had been no incest.

"Can I see the ticket? Do you have it with you?"

"No no I always keep it hidden don't want the other guys getting wrong ideas you know that's my ticket out of here; I've got to keep it safe,"

"It's got—money in the safe,"

"Yeah, loads of money, all sorts of money, enough to buy me a private institution like this if I wanted with my own gardens and staff,"

"Well that's awesome Rene,"

"Yeah; yeah I'm real excited; it's got documents too, to ensure I get the money,"

"Good, that's good. I'm sure you will, but it's always good to safeguard. You know, the uh—sometimes on weekends in the residential programs they let you out for a—vacation—"

"Yeah, yeah I know,"

"And I heard you're going to have a hearing later today? Maybe they'll release you to—ah, where was—" Norman searched his notes to find the name of the psychiatric hospital from which Rene had originally been transferred.

"Yeah, yeah Collins, Collins is where they'd take me to; they're taking me there later this afternoon. I'm real excited, I think I've got a chance; they don't want me to know about how influential my family is but my uncle likes me now he's different than the rest he's not in on it all, he wants me to know about them see. He's letting me in because he knows I can handle it. It's very important. Not everyone can, you know; it's a big responsibility knowing; they could just decide to get rid of me—get me out of the way—"

"Are you worried they might try that? Do you feel threatened?" Usually Norman's conversations with patients remained strictly confidential. But delusions that caused patients pain he felt liable to bring to the attention of psychiatrists who were better equipped to help counter them.

"No no I'm just saying they could; I'm not worried they would; see, once I let everyone know, they can't get rid of me,"

"Know—about your uncle's high up position at Servways?"

"Yeah, yeah, board of directors and not just Servways; he can draw from all kinds of different psychiatric facilities. Now you've gotta remember they've got loads of things they're trying to do; you have to watch out for the pigeons; you have to kill the pigeons; they're not pigeons they're spy drones remember that they spy on you for my uncle, my uncle's really high up, he's very influential,"

"The pigeons?"

"Right, yeah, the pigeons; they've got lasers in their eyes for cyber-optic cameras that go straight to their brain and those relay back to my uncle, but he's given me the ticket see, because now he finally wants me to know; but he didn't let anybody see, because that'd subvert the system; it has to be secret it can't go through the mailing shoots 'cause here they don't know about how he controls everything; they don't know about it but my uncle wants it all out in the open—that's why he's instructing me,"

"With the ticket?"

"Yeah,"

"About the birds?"

"Yeah, the pigeons, they have lasers in their eyes which lead back into optic nerve cameras, you know, you have to be ready for the optic nerve cameras you have to make sure you can outsmart them,"

Norman wrote down 'optic nerve cameras.' "You know I think that kind of technology would actually be pretty useful in a sting operation—"

"Yeah see now you're thinking like him, that's good; now you're thinking like him; that's why he uses them, all the time; it's always a sting operation; they're always watching, yeah; you've got that police stuff, I like that,"

Rene was agitated today; he kept shifting forward to slide his chair closer to the table. Norman could tell he was anxious about the upcoming hearing.

"So, if they decide you can be let out on good behavior, you get—"

"Yeah bumped to the lesser security yeah,"

"And then, 6 months probationary period and if you pass that—"

"Yeah, yeah I know a normal prison," (to account for the fact he'd broken an innocent man's ribs), "but I don't think I'm gonna like that I don't think they can hold me there,"

Patients often felt they were better off in some sort of institution, "I like it here; I can stay here, that's why my uncle gave me the ticket,"

"So, you'd like to stay at Servways?"

"No no I mean I want my old room back, you know, I want my old room back,"

"But just, still at a facility,"

7

"Yeah, yeah exactl;y I like the facilities,"

"Well I'll miss you if you do transfer,"

"Oh, I'll tell you; I'll let you know; my uncle can tell you too, and besides it'll be a while processing after the hearing,"

"Right, good, okay; and you'd be transferred to Collins? That's not too far away,"

"Yeah yeah well, Collins is where they take me, yeah,"

"Awesome. Alright, that's not bad. Although, you know, if you do want a chance at your old room back—I might not tell them about the ticket—it might look—bad?—"

"Oh, it subverts the system, I know, that's because my uncle's at the head of the system, right? So, they're gonna have to let me out,"

"Yeah,"

Norman had meant, more, they might find the return of this divisive illusion a cause for concern. What if some other patient should similarly claim, once again, that the ticket didn't exist?

"But you wouldn't—mm. I'm just worried they'll find that disconcerting,"

"Oh no no I'm not gonna punch anyone again I've learned my lesson,"

Norman's face split into a grin. "That's what I was worried about; I'm so glad,"

"Oh yeah no no that was really more about power dynamics; he was claiming my uncle wasn't head of Swervways and I was saying, 'no you don't understand,' but now I see my uncle has to keep it that way, otherwise outsiders may know,"

"Oh yeah, no, that makes sense,"

"Yeah yeah, I know how to play it now, no worries,"

"Good. But you will let me know how it goes?"

"Oh yeah yeah, I can put you down for next Tuesday, does that work?"

"Yeah, next Tuesday sounds great!"

CHAPTER 2

The hearing took place only a few yards down the street from the unit where Norman met Rene. Norman could see the Brutalist concrete side-ribbing of Collins Hospital when he returned to the parking lot thirty minutes later, swinging in to his car to go drive to the nearest cafe for a croissant and a coffee before picking up groceries and heading home. That was his routine, now he was retired.

As for Rene, the rest of the day passed slowly, but fretfully. He spent a great deal of time watching sunlight move across the linoleum floor by the chair in which he habitually waited for the dispensary to open at 2 for afternoon medications. There were programs for learning how to paint, but Rene hadn't wanted to settle into life here at Servways; he wanted out.

At 2 pm two orderlies in white beckoned him over. He had already put on a blue fleece, to prepare him for what might be cold weather outside; he hadn't bothered to walk out into the exercise yard to find out.

"You ready?"

"Yeah,"

"A little nervous?"

"Very,"

"It'll be fine; you've shown significant improvement while you've been here, yeah?"

"Good luck Rene!" a passing dispensary nurse waved after them.

"Thank you," he could barely turn to look at her for more than a second; his ability to take in his surroundings had been so completely overruled by the sudden swipe back of cool air from the official, automated exit at the end of the visitor's area.

A cop car was waiting. Blue and black stripes. "Alright." The attendants out here were slightly less friendly. One was already strapped in by her seatbelt to the passenger side's front seat. She only glanced back when he got in. The other signed paperwork, then drove in silence, their car shortly submerged in the underground garage just dipped down beneath the side of Collins' super-structure Norman had been looking at.

They drove down one level, to park by a door where they were met by orderlies from the hospital. This was the official, automated entryway to a radiology department; Collins provided care as a general hospital as well; the psychiatric ward was only one floor.

From the radiology basement, Rene was taken to a back set of service elevators, to keep him separated from routine out-patients.

The orderlies pressed the button for floor two. This was a purely bureaucratic level made of green carpet tiles, and plastic bumpers leading down a maze of walls. Occasional scuffs on the wall promised one deliverer or another had overshot their mark upon attempting to maneuver treatment carts round the hallway's intermittent, sharp corners.

Rene's hearing took place in Room 307-b.

A panel of doctors and lawyers had set up folding tables to one side to oversee the proceedings. Rene himself was accompanied by his own legal advisor, ensuring due process guaranteed Rene's rights. Facing him, the main doctor, whose decision as to whether Rene was ready to inhabit a less secure unit would be final, smiled pleasantly over a cup of water.

"How are you doing?" he asked as soon as Rene sat.

"Alright,"

"Good. Now, this is nothing to worry about, we are just going to ask a few questions to see how you are getting along in your new environment, and whether an extension to your stay is necessary, or not needed. And, we would like to hear your input, as to whether or not you think you would like to stay in the more secure unit, or if you would prefer to be transferred, in a process that would take a few weeks, to a resettlement in this facility, in our center known as the Lacktown Wood Unit for Psychiatric care. They've just had an inpatient opening there. As I'm sure doctors Dupont and Speritz have explained to you, this would begin an evaluation period of six months, at the end of which, should you wish to petition again for a hearing, you may have the option to remove to a standard correctional facility for processing under purely penal regulations, alright?"

"Yeah,"

"So, what we'd first like to establish is whether you would like to stay at the Servways Protective Facility, or if you think you might be ready to be transferred to Lacktown for psychiatric processing,"

"I'd like to be transferred,"

"Alright, and ah, can you tell us a bit about the evaluations you've undergone while you were at Servways?"

The responsibility for tabulating the records of tests, therapies, and treatments Rene had found helpful rested with the legal advisor who sat to Rene's right, but he had only just opened his files when Rene started right in.

"Well I've found talk therapy very helpful,"

The lead doctor found that interesting.

"I've especially enjoyed the volunteer program where you can talk with volunteers; I've got a friend who I've been meeting very frequently and we were just discussing how I know I shouldn't have lashed out at the other member of my psychiatric ward when he was patronizing about my uncle's privilege, because I wasn't even supposed to know about my family's influence, since it's based on gaming the system of private prisons, but I'm gonna be able to prove once I'm out that this is the case, because I have the ticket my uncle entrusted to me which will prove, with the money he's left me, that I was right, and my friend was telling me not to talk about the ticket when I came here—"

"Is this the same ticket that caused the initial altercation at--?" the head doctor looked up the name of the original psychiatric ward Rene had been transferred out of, "—Wesley?"

"No, it's a new one; he sent me a new one; that's how I know he's meant for me to find it; he wants me to know about the proceedings and my friend said there's no way he could get me the ticket because he couldn't get it past the mail guards and I didn't get mad, I said just calmly that my uncle doesn't need the mail guards; he can bypass the mail security,"

This attitude actually did show great improvement in Rene's mental well-being. The line of three doctors to Rene's left was, however, slightly concerned about the discussion he had had with a friend who had advised him not to tell the hearing's officials about his newly acquired belief he had somehow regained the ticket he claimed his uncle kept sending him.

He wasn't supposed to mention that ticket to anyone.

"Yes, well that's very good; we might be able to see what we can do— ah, if not necessarily a transfer to Collins Lacktown, certainly another rehabilitation center in the near future."

11

CHAPTER 3

Rene left the hearing feeling very pleased. "I think it went well, I really think it did," he told the orderlies from Servways who met him at the hospital's exit to the garage, below ground.

"You think they'll okay you for the residential program then?"

"Yeah, they had an opening—"

"Excuse me," two orderlies in blue descended down the ramp that led to the parking lot's exit. "Are you Rene Cartesius?"

"Yes?"

"You need to come with us now—" one of them took hold of Rene's arm.

"Sorry, no wait— who are you—?"

"We're high security unit personnel; this man's—"

"We're high security unit personnel." The security team from Servways assured. "From just across the way—"

"Yes, if you could please, just step aside, we don't want anyone to get hurt,"

"No—sorry—where are you taking him?"

"We're transferring Mr. Cartesius to the Freemont-Lowell Center for Psychiatric Care—"

"What the—?"

"If you could just sign the order forms here—"

"No, I don't—"

"Yeah, we need to make a call, what is this?"

Norman, meanwhile, had finished his croissant, and was just returning from buying 3 halibut fillets, mushrooms, tomatoes and asparagus.

He remembered Rene's hearing had been at 3pm, and swung into the parking lot, just to ask Fred Bently at the door whether Rene seemed to think his interview had gone well upon returning back through to his accommodations.

"Hey, Fred? Rene said he had that important rehabilitation hearing today at 3pm; let me know if it's too confidential, but—did he seem happy with the results when he came back through here? I was in the area, thought it'd be worth an ask,"

"Eh, they haven't actually come back yet,"

"O-oh," it was five o'clock now. "Well hopefully that's a good sign,"

"I guess?"

"I know he kind of had his heart set on getting his old room back—do they do that? Do they let patients return to their old rooms? I feel like that'd be a good idea to foster stability,"

"Ah, I wouldn't know,"

"Well, at least the same facilities then,"

"Ah no not for Rene, I'm afraid; he came from Wesley Crown--that's the hospital just two miles south of Aderlay; they're full up for now, but the Collins Institute had an opening at their center,"

"Oh, I see I must've gotten that—confused," Norman made a mental note to add that to his binder of notes; now he couldn't be sure which hospital Rene had been hoping to be admitted into. He'd have to ask next Tuesday, if Rene didn't mind him knowing, of course.

He was just exiting again when he saw Rene himself, across the street, in the grip of two orderlies in blue, walked up to a waiting black Bugatti Veyron—in fact, the same Bugatti Veyron that had earlier that morning been parked outside the Servways Facility.

Hugh Cossimer could be seen briefly, shaking hands with Rene before both descended within the confines of the car, taking one orderly along with them and leaving the other to head back down into the Collins Hospital garage.

Norman let himself down into his own car, feeling this must mean the hearing had in some way been successful. Trips off site were usually only granted to residents of less secure psychiatric wards, so, maybe, Rene had already been vouchsafed the privileges that came with being accepted into Collins' psychiatric unit.

Imagine getting to go for a drive one on one with Hugh Cossimer. Norman grinned. He hadn't known Rene was a Cossimer fan.

CHAPTER 4

Only two days later, Norman received a phone call. His land line still coiled an overly long cord along the side of his kitchen's entryway, so that he had to get up from where he'd been sipping coffee over a crossword puzzle while peeling potatoes.

"Yes, hello?"

"Is this Norman Cromel?"

"Yes, this is he?"

"This is Wade Ferner from the check-in center at Servways,"

"Oh no, did I miss an appointment?" he almost doubled back to check his scheduler.

"No; I'm sorry to have to tell you this, but I've been notified that Rene Cartesius—the patient you saw—"

"Yeah, of course—"

"He recently passed away; we got the news just this morning."

A slightly cockney accent had called it in early at 6 am.

"Oh; oh my goodness. Am I allowed to know what happened?"

"It was a suicide, I'm afraid. I'm so sorry; I know you two had gotten along pretty well,"

"Oh no— I'm— I'm so sorry. I had no idea he was doing that bad,"

"It was kind of sudden; they transferred him to a Freemont-Lowell Center for Psychiatric Care just after his hearing; I think they must have picked up on the fact something was wrong,"

"Oh," that name sounded familiar, somehow.

"Anyway, um, some of his old belongings are still here, at Servways, we were wondering if you might like to take a look through them? I know you're due tomorrow to talk with Mark; do you want me to leave them aside for you? Pick out a memento?" They'd be incinerated otherwise.

"Yes, yes please; that would be lovely; thank you so much for thinking of that,"

"Yeah, of course. I'm so sorry to have to tell you. I don't think any of us saw it coming,"

"No, no I can't believe it," Norman felt personally responsible. As a volunteer visitor, he was meant to cheer the men inside the secure unit. If only he'd thought to take a course, some form of training specifically for recognizing suicidal ideation. It simply wasn't a contingency that presented itself frequently. The patients at Servways were often depressed, but seldom actively suicidal. Usually Norman's fears ranged more towards concern for his own safety when he met with new inmates, though nothing had ever happened to exacerbate concerns.

He went back to peeling potatoes without doing his crossword, too old to be thoroughly shaken, simply sobered.

He did feel a twang of sadness, though, as to the sudden end to his short acquaintanceship with Rene, the next day, upon opening his binder at random while waiting to talk with Mark and finding the notes from his last session with the young man.

He turned to a blank page quickly, recalibrating to be able to give Mark the attention he deserved.

"Mark! How are you?"

Once the interview ended, he went to look through the few belongings of Rene's that Wade had kept back for him behind the front desk: a track suit, fake dog tags without any necklace to sling round a neck, shower slippers, a bottle of Vaseline, and the tote bag he'd brought on the first night of his admittance from his old residential psych ward — Wesley Crown, Norman supposed. The act he could remember its name accented his grief.

"I might take the dog tags," he told Wade, "thank you." They seemed to illustrate Rene's personality well, somehow—a bit of a renegade. Norman pat his way absent-mindedly through folding the duffle bag back into the small bundle Wade had stored it as.

In a pocket down the side was a luggage room ticket, for locker 264. Now how had—?

Norman put on his reading glasses to make sure he hadn't been spooked by a laundry list.

No, it was a ticket from the luggage room at the local train station; Norman would recognize it anywhere. For five years towards the end of his stint as Inspector, his beat had ended every Saturday just by WestEnd train station. He used to take the train up to Brightmol to visit his sister for dinner. The ticket's digital time stamp was less than a week old.

"Sorry, Wade?"

15

"Mm?"

"Did Rene ever go on any trips outside the secure unit, during the time he was here?"

"You mean visiting relatives? Or other units?"

"Just— outside the compound?"

"Naw, 'fraid they don't let you out all that often here."

"So no trips?"

"No, no, Collins for the hearing—but that was his first time out since he arrived,"

"Did he receive any visitors, other than me?"

"No, wasn't here long enough for that, I guess,"

"And you said he didn't receive any mail?"

"That's right,"

"You're sure?"

"I can check—?"

"Yes please,"

The letters and parcels orderlies processed were logged in Servway's online databases, so families could be sure their relatives inside received mail. Norman waited while Wade scrolled through the system's back log.

"Did he ever tell you about a ticket his uncle gave him?"

"Oh yeah; the luggage room ticket?" Wade seemed vaguely dismissive. He hadn't noticed Norman had found a scrap of paper.

Norman showed it to him.

"It's dated 3 days ago,"

"What the—?"

"And I didn't bring it to him. Could one of the orderlies have snuck it in?"

"I don't—" if they had, that constituted a breach in protocol. Orderlies weren't supposed to encourage patients' delusions. Seeming confirmation of Rene's obviously idealized interpretation of his own relationship with his uncle, so easily proven later to have been unfounded, could very well have contributed to Rene's passing. Wade realized this could mean a lawsuit while his mouth was still opening to say a response he now decided might best be kept quiet. "Noo, I don't think anyone'd do that. Someone else woulda noticed; we police each other as much as the patients you know. Maybe, ah, the entry system just didn't record a visitor,"

That would mean, Norman reasoned, that whoever gave Rene the ticket could potentially bypass Servway's Secure Unit's protocols. Wasn't that precisely what Rene had said his uncle could do?

Norman tried to read what was going through Wade's mind. Why had he clammed up so suddenly?

From twenty-one years on the police force, Norman knew not to show his hand, when something didn't add up. He pocketed the ticket, trying to play off his concerns casually. "Guess I should have taken him more seriously. It's too bad." He'd keep the ticket, even if only to remind himself not to take delusions too lightly. "Where'd you say they transferred him? Freemont-Lowell?"

"Yeah, Freemont-Lowell— just up north near Freeport,"

"Mm. Do you suppose they'd let me pay my last respects?"

"They might,"

"I just feel responsible, you know?"

"No, no don't think that way; there wasn't anything anyone could've done. You really did help him while he was here,"

"Thank you,"

Wade was simply relieved Norman seemed to have forgotten about the ticket's discrepancy.

"You'll keep the dog tags then?"

"Yeah. Can I keep the sweater too? He always said it was—well, too good for this place," Norman laughed. Rene had never said anything of the kind, but it was a nice blazer with red stripes up the sleeves. "Do you think they'll let friends see the body? Say goodbye?"

"It's worth a shot,"

Norman just wanted the finality of making absolutely certain Rene's suicide really had been self-inflicted—then he could feel comfortable accepting the ticket he held in his pocket was just some easily explained result of a dispenser set to the wrong time. He'd been a cop for far too long not to be bothered by the fact he'd failed to report Rene's concerns someone was out to get him. And then, Rene himself had died. After all, Wade had said they transferred him instantly to Freemont, soon as the hearing was over. That was against protocol. Protocol required two weeks' holding.

CHAPTER 5

Freemont Lowell Center for Psychiatric Care was only a thirty-minute drive from Servway's Protective Facility, a modernist brick Colossus that made up for the regimentation of inpatient's windows on its left wing via an entryway made almost entirely of glass.

As soon as Norman saw it, he remembered why the name had sounded familiar. It must have been four years ago now, an inmate from the woman's High Security Unit within Servway's system had befriended him for a good seven months, meeting up every Thursday to chat before the therapy sessions and pharmacological treatments Servways provided had been enough to get her 'stepped down' to Freemont's evaluation center.

Frances had been transferred to Servway's secure unit as the perpetrator of violent stalking. It was obvious from speaking with her only a few minutes that she ought not to be forced back into the population of a general prison to fend for herself, but she'd probably never be able to leave the facilities provided by one psychiatric program or another. She'd seemed comfortable at Freemont, though. Norman had visited her once, after her transfer. They'd been preparing to transfer her again, from the evaluation unit to more permanent accommodations in Freemont's residential program—the same type of program Rene had been hoping to enter.

The place felt nice; Norman remembered Frances' mental health had certainly stabilized.

It was easy enough for him to find his way again to the help desk. But he knew enough about hospital protocols he was fairly certain Wade's optimism, when it came to assuming they'd let unrelated members of the public view a body, had been unfounded. He would have to be clever about this, if he had any hope at all of actually viewing Rene's remains.

"Hello," he donned an innocently bland expression. "I'm a Visiting Patients volunteer at the Servways Centers for Psychiatric Development, and I was told a friend of mine was recently transferred here?"

"Name?"

"Rene Cartesius,"

The attendant searched through their computer files.

"Oh. Yeah this might be a bit of a special case. Let me get you a conference room; and, someone will be in to discuss things with you in a little bit, okay?"

Norman nodded, playing along. He hoped that if they believed his bereavement sudden, they may be more likely to let him view the body, as a means of placating him, avoiding upset.

They led him aside, careful not to seem too mysterious.

The doctor chosen to perform the sensitive task of letting Norman know his friend was dead was about 30 years old and came in rubbing sanitizer over his hands.

"Hey, thank you for waiting," he sat down. "I'm so sorry to have to tell you this, but Rene actually passed away yesterday." Norman tried his best to emulate the descending weight of emotions that might come from having genuinely waited in concerned ignorance. The doctor nodded. "Yeah, it was very sudden." He'd only had time to read what had happened on a generalized memo he'd received two minutes before entering the conference room with Norman. "We think he somehow managed to get ahold of an article of clothing he had with him, and, unfortunately, used that to end his own life. Of course, we can't just have the patients walking around naked. He was showing significant improvements at his last facility—"

"Servways—"

"Yes, that's right. And he had asked at a hearing just the day before to be allowed greater freedoms of movement, a privilege he showed every indication of being able to handle. Sometimes, especially with very intelligent patients, this sort of thing just happens, and, you know, they're clever enough to know what the system's looking for, and, when patients are determined to act a certain way, even trained professionals can't tell the difference between someone whose pretending to feel healthier, and someone who is actually healthier,"

Odd how Wade had assumed the sudden transfer to Freemont-Lowell had been in response to concerns Rene had taken a turn for the worse. If Norman's memory did serve him well, and policy did dictate transfer to lower security units took two weeks to finalize, that could account for why Wade had assumed an emergency; he was trying to think up some reason why they hadn't followed bureaucratic procedure, as was Norman. And now here was this doctor saying there had been absolutely nothing out of the ordinary, when it came to monitoring Rene's mental health. The transfer, in fact, signaled a routine step in the right direction. Was he trying to cover up the fact they had somehow mismanaged an emergency?

Norman kept silent; his face stony, inscrutable. "Can I see the body?" his voice actually did break, on this note. "Say good-bye?"

"Aah… yes I can see if he's still on-site. Usually, we transfer patients post-mortem to a morgue—"

"Which morgue?"

"Uh—Sanisburies?" The quickness of the question in the midst of what ought to have been shocked sadness took the doctor by surprise. Was Norman really that intent on making one final visit to his friend? Perhaps a slight hint of senility, the doctor worried. Ah, well. It wasn't like talk-therapy volunteers knew enough about the hospital's private system of morgues to be able to locate Sanisburies based solely on the abbreviated name staff called it by. "But, um. As his death was recent, he may still be on site. I'll go check for you. Would you like that?"

"Yes, please. Thank you. I'll come with you,"

"Right,"

The doctor let Norman leave the room first, nodding as he passed, then took the lead to bring him back to an information desk farther in the psychiatric facility's bowels, past the conference rooms for visitors.

"Marnia? This gentleman was wondering if he can see the body of his friend? A Mr. Rene Cartesius? I told him the body may still be on site. Can you check?"

The doctor turned back to Norman. "Okay, all good?"

"Yes, thank you,"

"Again, I'm so sorry to be the bearer of bad news; please feel free to stay as long as you want; we've got a cafeteria on the fourth floor,"

"Thank you, thank you,"

They shook hands and the doctor departed.

"Alright, a—uh, you said Rene—?"

"Cartesius, that's right,"

"Ah, it looks like we don't have his body in our facility anymore; we usually transfer them to a larger morgue after its been about a day,"

20

"Mm." An old policeman's tactic came to mind. "Can you find out where he went?"

"Oh, I'm sorry sir, those records are confidential,"

"Oh, okay. You can't—tell me where my friend went?"

"No, I'm sorry. I would get in contact with his family—"

"I don't know his family,"

"Mm. Well, they're'll be an announcement in the local paper for his funeral, I'm sure. That should be able to tell you everything you need to know."

She didn't seem overly guarded. If there was some discrepancy in Rene's sudden transfer to Freemont, it must not have been abnormal enough to arouse administrative concern. Ai, what a waste of a trip.

"Alright, thank you." Norman tapped the desk with his knuckles in lieu of saying goodbye, then doubled back. "Ah, do you have a Frances Hayworth still staying at these facilities, by any chance? She came about four years ago; I used to be her conversation partner for the visitor volunteer program?" Might as well see if she was still around.

"Frances—? Uh," the nurse noted Norman's visitor volunteer badge. The program's strict vetting process entitled him to freer access to knowledge about patients than would otherwise be given out to the public. She typed a moment. "Yes; she's just at the monthly fair for visitors right now, actually, would you like to go see her?"

"Yes please."

The monthly fair for visitors had to be tightly controlled; only a few patients were allowed to participate at a time. At Freemont, only one unit of the residential psychiatric ward was allowed to participate each month. They used a rotating schedule, for who would get to enjoy the fair when. Seemed it was Frances' unit's turn.

A similar games-day was arranged once every six months at the High Security Units, to get patients interacting with others they might not ordinarily see, but for high security patients, visitors weren't allowed to participate.

Allowing family members to come take part, and cheer on their children or spouses, Norman sensed, would add an entirely new dimension to the strain these fairs put on hospital staff.

He was led back past a series of examination rooms for routine check-ups for long-term in-patients, down past a laundry depository's hallway, and finally down steps to a more open, glass enclosed atrium that led out to the back of the asylum's grounds.

Three white tents had been erected, to house egg-walking contests, pottery events, and other activities in which family along with in-mates could participate.

21

Again, had Norman not sported his visitor volunteer badge, he would not have been allowed entry. As it was, he was one of the few people present unrelated by blood to any of the patients.

A nurse led him over to a welcoming awning where family signed in and called over a loud-speaker: "Frances Hayworth, you have a visitor. Please report to the Welcoming Tent,"

"She's got her sister with her as well," a sitting orderly looked up Frances on a chart with rows of highlighted names, demarcating who had shown up amongst those pre-registered.

"Norman?" He turned to find the pair of them.

"Hey! I hope you don't mind me stopping by?"

"Of course not, what a lovely surprise," Frances' sister answered for her in a way the heady mix of antipsychotics Frances took disenabled.

"What are you doing here?" she blinked.

"I came by to see you!" He didn't want to admit Rene's death had made him lonely.

"Really?"

"Yeah, I hope that's okay,"

"Of course! I'm Natalie by the way,"

They shook hands.

"Norman,"

"Oh, I remember a Norman! Frances told me about you,"

"I was just telling her," Frances' words always came slow and slurred, an effect exacerbated by medication, "how they need to start getting us more talk therapy here; I really liked that,"

"Well, would you like me to come visit you here more often? I can do that, you know."

"They say I have to do a training course,"

"It's some sort of new protocol thing," Natalie explained.

"Before she's allowed to talk to volunteers?"

"No, for my medication,"

"Oh, I see,"

"They have a training program for the inmates, for greater security," Natalie tried to explain, but honestly, Norman felt he could make better sense out of Frances' usual laconicism.

"Do you think it's beneficial?" he asked as vaguely as he could, unsure, quite, what they were talking about.

"I haven't seen an increase in training," Frances shook her head.

"Yeah go figure." He grinned. He could at least tell, whatever it was, Frances thought it was stupid.

"—We were just about to go do the coin toss; do you want to come?"

"Sure; how does a coin toss work?"

"You just throw the coin," Frances hated it.

"You're trying to aim it into a little bucket," Natalie clarified.

It felt nice to be back with Frances, see an old, familiar face, meet new, kindly people like Natalie. The coin toss was at the far end of the monthly fair's grass enclosure, a section of the ward's usual ambulatory grounds that abutted more confined, fenced in dirt yards that could be used for exercise for inmates of the unit next door. These men would get to attend the fair next month, when their turn came. Now, they shuffled as per usual, backs bent to an extreme angle for several of them, moving in groups as orderlies shepherded them towards recreational therapy, which would today take the form of playing basketball.

Norman flipped his coin and lost.

"You get to try again if you want," Frances seemed to be flat-lining from boredom.

"Alright," he got out another coin—

"No, no, you've gotta use the coins from the game, sorry," an orderly handed him a new one.

"Okay," he got it into the bucket this time. "Hey! Success!" in the celebration of smiling, he happened to look up and over at some of the men from the neighboring unit who'd taken to watching the fair from the basketball court. Rene stood among them, watching him from the free-throw line. "Ren—hang on, one second okay?" Norman excused himself. "Hey! Hey!" he practically jogged to the fence— paining his old joints, to push a hand against its cool metal links.

He'd been wrong. It was Rene, but he hadn't been watching the coin toss; he'd simply gazed in the fair's direction a moment, bored with free-throws. Now he'd moved on to watching the intake tent. "Rene!" Norman shook the fence and beckoned. "Hey!"

Rene pointed at himself, questioningly.

"Yeah! Hey!" Rene didn't recognize him. Sometimes, medications could produce a stupor— "I have your ticket!" Norman realized, fumbling.

"What?" Rene drew closer.

Interactions between units were not so rare that the orderlies overseeing basketball wouldn't allow them. From Norman's casual clothing, he could almost have been an inmate—though his shoes had soles that were too stiff to be allowed in-patients. The orderlies relaxed a tad from where they'd sat up, but still kept a keen look out, as Rene jogged over.

"I've got your ticket," Norman batted round his jeans' pockets frantically now, to hold it up, finally. He pressed it to the gap between the fence's linkages. "Remember this?"

Rene snatched it from him through the fence and ate it.

"Hey what the—?"

"Rooky! Hey!" Norman's startled jump back alerted orderlies to the need to intervene. They rushed over, "Ay! Rookrook! Don't do that bud,"

Rene snatched his arm away from the orderlies.

"Alright, come on, come on—"

"Wait—" Norman tried—

"It's alright sir, just, try not to antagonize—"

"I was told he was dead!"

But by now, the orderlies were too busy calming Rene down: "naw, naw, it's alright, come on, it's okay— breathing exercises." They walked Rene back over towards the basketball court.

"Hey! Scuse me—!?" They either didn't hear Norman calling after them, or chose to ignore him, assuming he was some crazed heckler.

What the hell? They weren't even supposed to give patients nicknames unless they asked for them. Since when had Rene wanted to be called "Rooky"? Norman wasn't going crazy; that was definitely Rene. Same moles—

Frances came to join him.

"You knew him?"

"Yeah,"

"Yeah. He's different, now isn't he?"

"Yeah,"

"Yeah they cloned him. They're always cloning people in that unit."

"Oh."

Frances suffered from paranoid schizophrenia. This had to be a new delusion.

"They go in; they clone you; that's why he's unhappy. I can tell you more about it, but not here; they've got the birds here,"

"The birds—?"

"Yeah the pigeons; they're watching,"

Had bird drones suddenly become a common delusion?

Rene had mentioned that delusion too!

Maybe staff members had failed to vet a particular book that'd managed to make its way into inmates' communal libraries at both Servways and Freemont; some new popular best-seller.

The concept of surveillance pigeons almost irritated Norman, he was so flustered from seeing Rene alive and well.

What on earth?!

That had definitely been Rene. He walked the same! Loping….

24

"Can you request me as a volunteer to talk to?" he returned his attention back to Frances. "I'm interested,"

"About the clones?"

"Yeah,"

He'd conducted enough police interviews to know conspiracy theories, though poorly argued, could still contain clues as to the truth behind a mystery.

"Yeah I can request you,"

"You don't need some special training before you see visitors—that was just for the medication?"

"Yeah, that's just for medications,"

"Okay, good."

He led her back over to the coin toss. Rene had returned to playing basketball.

What the hell was that? Some breach in form?

Had Norman done something wrong? He was sensitive enough to instinctively assume that could be it. Were they purposefully trying to limit his interactions with Rene? Perhaps he shouldn't have suggested Rene fail to mention his delusions regarding the locker room ticket.

But claiming suicide? That was a bit harsh, no? It wasn't like bureaucracy needed to be deceitful, when it could so easily be purposefully obtuse instead.

But they wouldn't make a mistake about a patient committing suicide, for Christ's sake! Perhaps he ought to report— or was this some sort of confidentiality problem?

He allowed his attention to be steered back towards the coin toss once more.

"So, you can come visit again?" Natalie hadn't noticed anything strange happen; she'd been too busy helping one of Frances' fellow patients. "I know she'd love that."

"Oh, I'd love to,"

"Do you want to come Wednesday?"

"Sure,"

Norman penciled it in.

Once Frances needed a nap, he said goodbye and headed back to Freemont's central help desk.

"Excuse me? There's a patient in the ward abutting the communal grounds being used as a fair right now—goes by the name of Rooky or Rookrook; and I think I used to volunteer with him as a visitor's volunteer at Servway's high security mental health facilities; is there any way you can tell me if his name is Rene Cartesius?"

"Oh, I'm sorry sir, if you don't already know we can't give out that information,"

Norman's privileges as a visitor-volunteer only extended so far.

"I just, wanted to know if maybe he had a brother? It's just he's recently deceased; I only found out about it a day ago, ah...."

"Well we would certainly tell a patient if his brother had passed away, don't worry," she nodded, obviously wanting Norman to go away himself.

CHAPTER 6

As soon as he returned home from Freemont, Norman acted on the previous help desk nurse's advice and searched three separate local newspapers for any hint of an obituary for Rene. He was a pensioner; he had all the time in the world. But twelve different local newspapers didn't help him find a single hint of Rene's family, or the location of his final remains or last rights. Now Norman wanted to know what was happening. He'd have to get in contact with Rene's family somehow, he supposed. The Cartesius family, who never visited…. He supposed he could go to the census bureau. What he really wanted now was a death certificate.

And why the hell was that ticket—? Why did it exist? Why had Rene eaten it?! For God's sake—

In the meantime, his Wednesday meeting with Frances rolled round. The residential psychiatric unit where she stayed in Freemont-Lowell proved almost identical to that of the Secure Unit in Servway's. The only difference was that the hallway of doors that led into patients' rooms wasn't locked shut during the day. Patients were free to come and go and were each provided with a key to lock the door to their own room as they saw fit.

The room Norman was ushered in to to await Frances doubled as a reading room during the day and was in fact located within the hallway that housed the locked doors to patients' individual rooms.

It was interesting being able to see this more intimate, personal side to psychiatric patient care. The bunks, bolted down as Norman had always been told they were. The cast-off sweatshirts Norman hadn't expected would be allowed inside individual patients' rooms.

Frances came in smiling, personalized key-lanyard in hand. Everything was so much less official. Until they closed the door to their conference room. Then Frances sat down, scooted forward: "so, you wanna hear about the cloning?"

"Yes please,"

Norman had his pencil and paper out ready and waiting.

"Alright, so—what do you want to know?"

"Mm. I guess what exactly is the process behind it? Do you know?"

"Yeah, they clone people; they've got a special room for it below the prison,"

"Which prison?"

"This, the facilities. They talk about it like it's another unit, 'oh we're transferring you to another unit,' 'we're gonna take you to the unit now,' 'we're going to the unit,'"

"Who? Who talks about it?"

"Just anybody. Orderlies. People in charge,"

"Have you ever seen someone who seems like they might be in charge of it all? Someone you don't recognize from usual interactions?"

"Yeah. Oh yeah. They have celebrities in on this; Hugh Cossimer came by, just the other day,"

Norman tried to tell himself the fact Cossimer actually was the last person he'd seen Rene alive with could just be a coincidence. The famous actor did a lot of volunteer work. Very likely Cossimer was the only well-known name associated with the visitation program—so if Frances had wanted to make her delusions sound important, Cossimer's name might make an obvious choice to pick to associate with her fantasies.

"And—what does he use the clones for?"

"I dunno,"

"Do you know what other people might use the clones for?" he was trying to look for any sort of pattern, within her delusion, that might point to a truthful clue.

"I don't know; I never see them," she seemed to take offense at the question.

"Who do they clone? Would they clone you?"

"Oh yeah, yeah all sorts go down—and they come back up, as long as they're on the right side of the bars,"

"Who've you seen go down?"

"All sorts,"

"What about the most recent? The most recent person to be cloned?" If she was picking up on some sort of discrepancy in how certain patients were treated, she may not be that far off. Perhaps Rene's uncle really was high enough in command he could whisk a nephew away under false claims of suicide to a more comfortable facility. That wouldn't do.

"The most recent? I dunno; they come at night so the rest of us can't see; --once we're all locked in our rooms."

"Mm. So, what do they do? They come when you're in the—"

"Yeah, they take you out of your room; they unlock the door and take someone out; I can hear them, at night."

"Hm. So the night staff are in on it?"

"No, no, they bring in a special staff,"

"How can you tell?"

"I don't recognize the voices,"

"And you're sure this isn't just auditory hallucinations?"

"No no no mine talk to me; they don't shuffle—like," Frances scrubbed her feet across the carpeted floor to demonstrate.

"So, they take the patients away in the middle of the night?"

"Yeah,"

"Do they ever put up a fight?"

"No more than usual,"

"Mm. What door do they go out of?" Norman pointed to explain he meant the doors that lined opposing ends of the patient's hallway.

"That one," Frances pointed in the direction of the door that led out into the breakfast area Norman had walked through upon arrival.

"Hm." But that made no sense. "Surely processing would take place near more secluded areas, like the dispensary?"

The only place patients could be headed, if they headed out towards the cafeteria, would be towards the main doors that led to Freemont's side exit or towards the neighboring unit— where he'd seen Rene. "If they were being transferred, though, wouldn't they first need to—?" You'd think a final meeting with a psychiatrist would be in order. But that would take the patient back the opposite way, towards the dispensary.

"I don't know; I only know what I heard,"

It didn't seem to conform to normal protocol, at any rate.

"And they open that door?" he pointed, "you're sure?"

"Yeah, no they go out to the cafeteria area,"

"So, maybe they're going to another hospital?" out the side exit?

"I don't know,"

"Alright. That's interesting. Have you ever noticed if they tend to come at a particular time? Maybe there's a schedule?"

"Four am. Yeah. Wakes me up usually,"

"Do you manage to go back to sleep afterwards?" This question was simply genuine, personal concern. But it could also indicate whether or not she'd been dreaming.

"Sometimes,"

"Hm. And you're still taking that insomnia medication?"

"Yeah; the Noverone, only now they've bumped me up to 25mg."

"Did you tell anyone else about this?" Perhaps the increased medication dosage could be to ensure Frances didn't hear too much. Might explain why she had a special training session in order to take medication—he'd never heard of that before. But tampering with medications— while endemic, surely, to a certain extent— was certainly worth investigating.

Especially if bank accounts like Hugh Cossimer's were involved. Willing to pay out to ensure the comfort of whomever Hugh had come to visit—Rene, at least, was one of those lucky inmates. A friend? Willing to pay to ensure Rene lived in comfort, perhaps? Perhaps Rene's uncle truly was an influential man.

"No no course not I don't go talking to people nowadays, not after they started cloning,"

"Not even your fellow patients? You don't tell—"

"No, I never trusted those freaks anyway,"

"Frances! A lot of these people are really sweet!"

"Bunch of wankers."

"Oh no-o,"

"I get by with my sister to visit me, and you coming sometimes; thank you,"

"My pleasure,"

"Just, do me a favor, yeah? Sign up to visit again. So they can't make me disappear, see? They'd know it was a pattern; they don't want you to find the patterns,"

"You mean, if you disappear after talking to me, that means your disappearance is related with to this conversation?"

"Yeah; they don't want you to think like that. Will you sign up?"

Frances always had been shrewd when it came to self-preservation. Norman assured that he would.

He left analyzing what precisely he had gained. News of nocturnal changes in patients' assigned rooms? That sounded relatively normal. If only he could find out if that really had been Rene he'd seen, and not some—brother. *'Don't say clone,'* he told his worrying subconscious.

Should he call Servway's and tell them he feared a breach in confidentiality had occurred, giving away a patient's things when clerical errors mistakenly reported him dead?

Or was it not a clerical error? How far would someone go, to make sure another person was comfortable? It made no sense though; Rene had had a fairly good chance of being transferred to a place like this through normal bureaucratic channels in two weeks' time, unless he'd totally blown the evaluation hearing at Collins, said something stupid. Now more than ever Norman wanted the closure of being able to attend Rene's funeral. Why hadn't he been able to find a public announcement of his friend's death?

By this point in his thoughts, he'd walked far enough from Frances' unit back towards his car that he found himself by the very fence through which he'd seen Rene four days before. He had an idea. He doubled back. "Left my planner," he smiled at the orderly guarding the entry to Frances' unit.

It wasn't difficult to find Frances again; she was out in the commons area, reading a romance novel before a Process Group Session she would be forced to attend at 4:30.

"Do you know anyone in that unit across the way?" he asked inconspicuously. "The one that's behind the basketball courts, on the other side of the green, outside?"

"You mean the cloning unit?"

"Is that the cloning unit?"

"Yes."

Again, her delusion did parallel the particulars of irregularities Norman himself had noticed. He respectfully dipped his voice to a whisper, seeing as Frances had done the same.

"Yes,"

"I thought you said they cloned people underground?"

"No, that's just where they process you,"

"Oh, I see."

"Martha's over there; she's an orderly,"

"No, I was thinking more a patient's name; would anyone here know anyone from that unit?" he knew some recreational events were designed to intermix units, so people could meet others they didn't normally get to see. He tried to be sensitive to the needs of Frances' delusion. "Do you trust anyone enough to ask?"

Frances thought a moment. "Yeah. Egbert?"

Egbert was a centennial who had been in the residential facilities since 2002.

"Do you know anyone who's in that unit across the way by the basketball courts, behind the green?"

"Sure; Frank Manley, Robert Spencer,"

Norman couldn't be sure these names even mapped onto people who had ever truly existed in this reality, but it was worth a shot. If he asked to see Rene himself, he feared some internal, bureaucratic note would pop up on the screen, discouraging the interaction. After all, from Norman's point of view, Rene was supposed to be dead. But they'd let him through when he'd known to ask for Frances' name….

"Thank you; that's perfect," he returned to Frances, "I've signed up to see you two weeks from Thursday; is that early enough, do you think?"

"No, that's good; it'll give me two weeks they have to keep me around,"

"Well— don't worry so much about that, please. You'll be fine; I won't let anything happen to you. Ok? I promise. You can trust these people."

"Don't trust these people,"

"I won't tell them anything—you know, confidential, but—they're good people; you don't need to worry, okay? I would—let them in on what you know, okay? Tell them what you've been telling me, they can help figure out whether there's some alternative explanation,"

"You'll tell them!"

"No, I won't. –I won't, okay? I promise." That could only make Frances more mistrusting. "But you have to promise me not to do anything rash. Because, I kept another patient's secrets for him. And it didn't help him get better. Frances. Do you promise me you'll at least try to broach the subject—even if in just a roundabout way? With your psychiatrist?"

She nodded.

As Norman retraced his steps towards the neighboring unit by the basketball court, he began to wonder whether he really was well-cut-out for this job. He just seemed to make patients more nervous, playing into their darkest delusions. He only meant to carry on a conversation, usually. Look where that had gotten Rene. He had to remind himself this proclivity towards goading delusion could not have influenced Rene's decision to kill himself, not if Rene wasn't actually dead.

But maybe this whole mystery was a simple reaction to the guilt he'd felt on finding out about Rene's suicide; maybe grief was coloring Norman's judgment. Was he simply trying to exonerate himself? Now he feared he was egging Frances on in the wrong way too. He cheered himself with promises if he could find some explanation for his own worries that Rene seemed to have magically doubled, he could share them with Frances, to assure her cloning factions were not eliminating mental patients who knew too much.

He decided to tell an orderly about her fears. He'd call up once he got home, to ensure the tip-off remained anonymous.

CHAPTER 7

Norman smiled as politely as he could to the orderly who found him at the door to Frances' "cloning" unit.

"I'm here to see Frank?" Norman held up his credentials. "I'm a volunteer for visiting and conversation,"

"Frank who?"

"Oh, I can't remember—" (just in case Egbert had remembered the wrong name), "they just told me the guy's name was Frank? Something like Man—ley? Maybe? Frank Manley?"

"Yeah we have a Frank Manley, you'll need to check in at the front desk."

Norman had bet right: the front desk oversaw a communal waiting area, almost as wide as the unit's skyrise itself. He scanned the patients who milled past, trying to look absent-minded, as he kept an eye out for Rene. A nurse was just finishing filling out forms. At length, she looked up.

"Yes, how can I help you?"

"I'm here to see a Frank Manley? I'm a Visiting Patients Volunteer?"

"Do you have an appointment?"

"Yes, I should be scheduled for—" what time was it? "—5:30."

"Alright; I'm not seeing you pulled up here on the schedule, actually,"

"Well, I got the call just about an hour ago,"

"Alright; lemme just go check real fast; is this your first time visiting the rehabilitation unit?"

Is that what this unit was? Curing substance abuse, then?

"Yes, I think so," Norman tried to act as he normally would when first visiting a patient.

"Alright, I'll just need you to fill out some paperwork while I check with Frank that he actually did make a request; I'll be right back; you can sit anywhere you like,"

Norman took a clipboard and the registration forms she gave him and went to sit with his back to the entryway, giving himself a full view of as much of the communal rooms as possible.

Rene, though, didn't seem to be out and about. The greater freedoms residential communities allowed did mean he could have gone back to his room to lie down in private. 5:30—from what Norman knew of the secure units in Servways, that was almost time for dinner.

A bell rang.

The patients began cuing at a kiosk built into the communal room's side wall.

That would be evening medications, then. If Rene was in residence, he'd have to come out. He'd complained to Norman enough times about the Orthornene they made him take before dinner.

"Sir?" the nurse had returned. "I'm sorry but Frank didn't put in any request for a Norman—sorry, what was it again?"

"Cromel?"

"Yes, I'm sorry; he hasn't put in a request for any visitors today,"

"Oh. But I got the visitor's call," Norman clutched at his badge as though suddenly defensive, still scanning for Rene.

"I'm sorry; I don't know what could've happened,"

"Well, can you check again? Maybe he remembered wrong,"

"I'm sorry sir, but it's just before our dinnertime; we actually don't take visitors this late anyway,"

"But, you must— I mean, I drove all the way out here,"

Norman's pleas were beginning to attract attention from some inmates at the end of the medication line. They stared at him dolefully, no doubt not exactly enamored of the system that enabled doddery old men to remain their only point of contact with the outside world.

"I'm sorry sir. If you'd like, I can schedule you into our listings, so patients can see your name when they want to meet someone new?"

"But I drove all the way out...."

Still no Rene. —Norman would stall for as long as he could....

"Yes, I know; I'm sorry sir; I'm afraid though we're going to have to ask you to leave now; we're about to have dinner, and as you know we keep a very tight ship when it comes to keeping the patients comfortable,"

"But—maybe—could I just talk to Frank? I think—"

There—! He stopped mid-sentence.

He'd finally caught sight of Rene, craning over one of the patients stooped behind him in line, to catch a glimpse of the dramatics Norman was causing.

Two orderlies had appeared to help escort Norman out. "Oh no, no no now please I—"

"I'm sorry sir, but if you can keep your voice low and soothing; it really is for the best. I know we instruct you guys on a lot of protocols—but—" Norman wasn't listening.

He'd zeroed in on Rene's face. There was no scar. He saw it plain as day. He didn't have a scar over his left eye—the scar from the fight that had landed him in the high security unit at Servways in the first place.

"—Rene—?"

"Sorry sir?"

"I think I can see my friend Rene—"

"I'm sorry sir, no one on this floor goes by that name,"

The orderlies were starting to think Norman may have escaped from the geriatric unit.

"But—" Rene's look alike turned away. That was insane. An absolute double, save the scar. He even parted his hair the same way! Dammit all! That had to be— "Rene Cartesian, Cartesian?" In the fluster of the moment, he remembered Rene's last name wrong.

"No, I'm sorry sir,"

"Mm…"

The orderlies seized their chance at Norman's momentary uncertainty and steered him back out of the rehab unit.

"Now are you sure you'll be alright finding your way home again?"

"Oh yes, yeah it's fine,"

"We're so sorry you had to come all this way for no reason; we'll look into the cause for the confusion; and we'll put you on our volunteer list, alright? It won't happen again,"

"Yes, yes thank you," he shook them off and returned to the car park.

Maybe he wouldn't report just yet that Frances was having delusions the neighboring unit was cloning people.

Not that he thought they were cloning people of course. Just because he couldn't trust himself to remain sane sounding, were he to broach the topic of clones with a psychiatrist. He could just see it now—he had a nervous little tick of a laugh that would belie all attempts to sound natural.

Could that have been Rene's twin? Or just an insane coincidence of a doppelganger? If a twin, surely at the mention of "Cartesius" they would have taken pity on an old pensioner's confusion— though— Rene had always said he was a bastard, hadn't he? Suppose that man's last name differed from Rene's. Was it possible to retain such a strong resemblance between half-brothers? It was the only way Norman could explain the scar's disappearance.

Maybe it could even explain why "Rooky" had eaten Rene's baggage-claim ticket. Rene prized it as proof—a link to his uncle's love. 'Legitimate' family could get jealous. That hardly made sense—but add madness…. Medications did strange things to patients' minds.

What Norman needed to do now was have a look at census records, discover what family Rene might claim descent from. See if they had any record of a young man in that family around 24 years of age, as Rene had been.

If, somehow, Norman had been mistaken about the scar—and the ticket, along with Rene's removal to Freemont were part of some ploy to ensure he was more comfortable— some conspiracy to provide privileged treatment within state-wide psychiatric facilities— the census could help Norman on that count as well. Who better to sound out for information than the uncle who had allegedly provided Rene with the very luggage ticket that had been the one tangible eccentricity to the case that clearly delineated an oddity worth investigating?

Everything else, Norman could fit into a convenient narrative of bureaucratic contrivance. Or, at best, negligence.

The ticket, on the other hand….

The only problem was that Rene's scar certainly had been real. You couldn't fake that, not with orderlies overseeing Rene's movements every day. If they were relocating him, that wasn't part of the ploy; orderlies would rumple that sort of theatrics instantly. Besides, Norman himself had gotten a good look at that scar, many a time. Perhaps, at the rehab center, he had simply overlooked it? But he could have sworn—

Well, either way, if Norman could find the uncle who had sent Rene the ticket—he may be slightly closer to an explanation.

Luckily, he had a clue. He was glad he'd written it down: Rene's aunt's husband's brother's brother.

If Rene's mom slept with her sister's brother-in-law, and the allocation of an additional epithetic 'brother' had been one of Rene's habitually absent-minded turns of phrase, Norman had simply to find Rene's mother, from his birth certificate, to find Rene's mother's sister, to find who Rene's mother's sister had married, to find the names of this man's brothers.

If Rene's mother had instead had relations with the brother-in-law of her sister's brother-in-law—and Rene had forgotten to add in an 'in-law,' this could get fairly complex. But either way, the search would begin at the Civil Registration services he had often had to turn to, during particularly difficult investigations as an inspector.

He went to the census bureau.

The bureau listed Rene as having been predeceased by an Alfred and Laura Cartesius. A check in old marriage registries confirmed Laura Cartesius had once been Laura Fornier.

Laura Fornier had had a sister named Dorothy. Dorothy Fornier had married Jebadiah Monado. Jebadiah Monado had a sister, Norma, and two brothers: Gottfried and Wilhelm. Damn, that meant two possible uncles.

As far as potential lookalikes went, neither of these men had ever had any children, but Dorothy had a son listed, born around the same year as Rene—that meant the existence of a man about 24 years old, who looked like Rene, was at least possible!

The uncles could tell Norman.

Their names, Gottfried and Wilhelm, were searchable online in recent census records. The database showed both Jebediah's brothers were living in the same town, Robencrescent, about an hour and a half from where Norman himself lived. That wasn't too far.

Norman decided that he would call on these gentlemen first in hopes he wouldn't have to track down every single brother-in-law related to the Monado family as well, in an attempt to piece together who may have sent Rene that ticket.

CHAPTER 8

Robencrescent was a pleasant enough hillock of meandering streams for about 15 minutes past the first outcrop of incoming residential zoning. Then it merged into zig-zagging bus-lanes and department stores.

Norman's Megane began to swelter under the strain of low air-conditioner fluid. He had to pull in to a neighborhood grocery to ask the way to 37 Crescent Avenue, bypassing the row of flowers by the door to place his grubbily penciled-in map before the attendant and ask why none of the street names local zoning authorities had printed seemed to bear any resemblance to the streets he was finding.

He'd already thought up a way to win each uncle over, in an attempt to sound them out, see who was likely to have sent Rene the ticket, if, indeed, either man had actually done so.

He'd brought along with him the sweater and dog tags he'd taken from amongst Rene's personal affects. He'd offer the dog tags to the first uncle, the sweater to the second, as a show of amicability. He had a 50% chance of arriving at the house of Rene's kindly uncle first. Perhaps, if he approached as a friend, he could win this man's confidence.

He got out at last by the house he sought at 37 Crescent Avenue, taking the dog tags with him, to go knock on the door.

A 75-year-old man answered, frail, but alert. "Yes? Hello,"

"Hello, are you Gottfried Monado?"

"Yes?" Gottfried had the slightest hint of an accent, a lilting, questioning clip to the end of certain phrases.

"My name's Norman Cromel; I'm with the visiting patients volunteer program at Servway's Protective Facility. I got to know your nephew there,"

"Oh, yes."

"I heard about his passing, and I thought you might like some of his things; I brought   " Norman handed over the dog tags.

"Oh, oh how lovely thank you, yes, yes, that's very kind,"

"He always spoke well of you; he was a good friend. I've been feeling a bit lost actually, it happened so suddenly—I guess I wanted to apologize, I should've seen the warning signs sooner,"

"Ah, no no no," Gottfried seemed to realize he had been visited by a man who in fact needed therapeutic conversation, though his promises insinuated he was there to dole it out, where needed. "Why don't you come in? I can give you a pamphlet from the funeral,"

"Oh, thank you,"

"Yes, yes come on in. Thank you so much for bringing these," Gottfried pocketed the dog tags.

"Are you sure you'll be doing alright—without? I know he said you were getting up in years and I understand you kept in pretty regular contact—"

"Did Rene tell you that? Good. I'm glad he found it regular enough; I myself always thought I was a bit too lax in that department. Do you want some tea?"

"Yes please,"

Norman looked round. The townhouse itself, while cozy, was bare, a common introvert's settling into minimal photos but multiple keepsakes. An array of teapots dotted the ledge above the kitchen's oven.

"Yes, Rene was a good kid; don't know what could've come over him, with that fight,"

"Well, he always said he was defending you that day—although, I've been told he actually had two uncles? It could've—?"

"Ah yes, that's right, my brother lives just down the road,"

"But no one else really—ever cared so much to visit, Rene, as you did?"

"Oh I wouldn't say that; Rene always had fantasies his family was out to get him, but he was a good lad; we—tended to stay clear of him if we were worried about him; he had a tendency to lash out, not understand."

"Mm." Norman had heard that story many times. "He seemed so full of life, I can hardly believe it,"

"That's fairly common actually; an acceptance of coming death often allows patients to feel freer and happier than they have in months,"

"You're a psychiatrist yourself then?"

"Mm, both my brother and I —well, retired. It's been several years now of course,"

"That's interesting; you know, he always said you—or, maybe, your brother, were quite high up at Servways,"

"That's right. I was head of the board of directors for quite some time, before I retired."

"And Wilhelm? Your brother is Wilhelm, isn't he? Was he ever associated with the—psych wards?"

"Yes; Rene told you that?"

"Mm,"

"Yes, that's right. He's retired now too, of course,"

"Mm. Thank you," Norman accepted his tea, watching. For being friendly, Gottfried certainly didn't give out a lot of information.

"It's a stupid question but—did you ever manage to get any special treatment for Rene? You know, I don't know, sneak him in some sweets or something silly?"

"Oh no no,"

"He seemed to hope—"

"Ahh, but that'd undermine the therapy,"

"Oh, I see, yes that makes sense,"

Maybe the other brother had been the one to send the ticket, then.

"And I suppose you've—well, you were saying; you've had the funeral service then?"

"Ahh, I wish you could have come,"

"I couldn't find an obituary notice; I looked,"

"Oh, that's a shame; here, let me get you a copy of it; I have one somewhere; it'll say where he's interred,"

Gottfried went to where he'd filed Rene's obituary away in a side-drawer of his desk in the living room that abutted the kitchen's pantry-like eating corner.

"Yes, here it is; Mailton Cemetery; just out of town, do you know it?"

"I'm sure I can find it, thank you,"

"You just take the first left after main street; drive straight out; you can't miss it. Rene's in the family plot. The office can tell you where,"

"Mm. Thank you."

They sat a while in silence while Norman read the paragraphs written in Rene's memory.

"They are funny things, aren't they, dog tags?" Gottfried had been studying Norman's gift. "I suppose young people think it makes you look tough. But I've never seen one without a name chiseled into it,"

"Yes, I thought that was strange too," Norman grinned. "Did you send him those?"

41

"Oh no no; did try to call sometimes, I suppose—at least, before he went to the secure unit. Thought he could use a bit of a breather after that,"

"Mm. It is so hard, isn't it?"

Honestly, Norman couldn't tell if this was the kindly uncle Rene had mentioned or not. His words seemed loving enough. They certainly matched everything loving family members of other patients always said. A little bit—too well, if Norman was going to be suspicious about it. Too generalized, almost.

There was no warmth to the way he said things, as though Rene, like his obituary, had been filed away. But perhaps that was simply how Gottfried dealt with grief. That was understandable. Still, by the end of the conversation, Norman somehow didn't quite trust Gottfried enough to ask—though he knew he needed to:

"Eh, I know—Rene always claimed he was a bastard related to the family, not actually part of it—is that true?"

"Ah, if you can call such antiquated ideas truth," Gottfried batted the thought away, then rambled down the complexities of Rene's lineage.

"Did he have any half-siblings?"

"Ah, no, no. A few cousins, certainly,"

As Gottfried was a psychiatrist, Norman didn't want to tell him he'd seen what appeared to be an exact duplicate of Rene, sans scar. That sounded mad. But he had to try—

"I just—I saw a guy the other day who looked like him; it made me think," Norman tried to be extra careful to imply, by the ease with which he said this, that he had in no way mistaken the man for actually being Rene. That was sure to bring Gottfried's psychiatrics out.

"Ah, no no. No brothers I'm afraid, just Rene."

So, there went Norman's theory the man he'd seen was just a stepsibling—a look-alike.

Maybe, before he pried too much more, he should try meeting Rene's other uncle, see if he seemed a more likely contender for sending Rene that ticket—or helping him to a more comfortable ward. Something about Gottfried struck Norman as off.

He thanked Gottfried and eventually left, taking out, once he got in the car, instructions on how to drive from Crescent Avenue to Lamhurst Drive—where Wilhelm lived—which the grocery store attendant had helpfully provided.

Wilhelm wasn't home. Norman went to get a croque madame at a nearby cafe, then returned two hours later.

"Yes? What is it? What do you want?" Wilhelm had even more of an accent than his brother.

"Are you Wilhelm Monado?"

"Who are you?"

"My name's Norman Cromel; I'm with the visiting patients volunteer organization at Servway's Protective facility."

"Oh?"

"I knew your nephew, Rene; we were good friends; I'm—just calling to say I'm so sorry about his passing,"

"Mm." Wilhelm scowled questioningly up at him, peering into his eyes.

"And, ah. Servways allowed me to take a few of his personal affects, and I got to thinking, maybe you'd like one? I have a—sweater that was always Rene's favorite,"

"Mm." Wilhelm seemed disappointed. "Don't have need for a sweater. Thank you. Good day." he made to close the door.

"Ah—well, will you be alright on your own, now? I—Rene always said you two were quite close; he was worried about you getting around on your own,"

"I've hired help,"

"Alright. Well, if you'd ever like to talk, y'know, the visiting volunteers program has a—"

"No, no need, thank you—not one of those pansy hippies, dwells on feelings. You wanna go talk dope with crack-head murderers you can talk to volunteers, not me."

The door closed.

Hm. Norman felt he must be losing his policeman's ability to conduct efficient investigations.

He couldn't tell if Wilhelm's abrupt attitude had been simple contempt for his nephew or just orneriness from tired grief.

But it seemed if Norman was going to ask one of the uncles about Rene's ticket, he had no choice but to go back to Gottfried, regardless of how unsure he was he was accurately reading each uncle's reaction to their nephew's death.

'What a meddlesome bore I've become,' he thought to himself, as he drove back to Crescent Avenue. Ah, well. It was fun to illicit a reaction out of people once more. To see some life brought back into the eyes of those he interrogated, as they sought to understand his purpose, and guard their own.

"Gottfried? Sorry to come again; I've been thinking it over and I'd like to ask you a question I—didn't feel comfortable asking before."

"Oh?"

"Yes; do you mind if I come in again? Are you in the middle of anything? It's important,"

"No, of course, come on in,"

"Thank you. It's about a ticket Rene claimed either you or Wilhelm sent him, a few—well, about a week ago now, I suppose. A luggage ticket, for the WestEnd train station in Glover."

Gottfried's face remained blank, perhaps vaguely surprised.

"For locker 264,"

That seemed to get Gottfried's attention. Though it could only have been the fact Norman managed to remember such a specific fact from his nephew's convoluted claims.

"Oh, yes? Yes, he had that delusion,"

"Thing is, I've seen the ticket. After Rene's death, I found it in amongst his assets, when I got the, dog tags—" Norman gestured to where Gottfried had left the dog tags by the teacups.

"Hmph. Do you still have the ticket with you?"

"No, I'm sorry, I lost it."

"Hm."

"But if the locker had personal affects in it, I don't think he had gotten around to claiming them, last time we spoke, if that—helps, or is important. I can get some old contacts I know to open it for you, just fine—but, what I really wanted to know, was—the time stamp, on the ticket, corroborated Rene's claim that you or Wilhelm had given him the ticket after he had been admitted to Servways. But Servways' records don't show anyone visiting him, or giving him mail—or really, anyway he could've gotten his hands on that ticket; I'm sure you know, they're not allowed out without special dispensation and since it's high security—"

"Maybe an orderly gave it to him, some kind of nasty prank?"

"Yes, that's the thing; that's what I was thinking too," Norman needed to push Gottfried now, "and well, that could be very serious, you see, because—well, you can't just do that to a person and expect them to remain even-keeled—even, perfectly healthy people. I know it meant a lot to Rene, and I'm worried that kind of tampering—that sort of thing—it could've led to Rene's suicide. I mean, I wanted to know what your thoughts were; can we sue? There has to be some sort of recourse,"

"Oh no no no not sue surely,"

"But you can understand how serious it is as a psychiatrist, right? To say, 'oh your uncle loves you, enough he gave you this ticket' and to later, you know, who knows, take it all back—it'd be so easy for him to find out it was a lie—"

44

"Oh no no I—here," Gottfried decided, "listen. Let me let you in on a little secret. I knew Rene was doing poorly, and I—just wanted to cheer him up, so, like an old retired, fogey, I—sent him the ticket. I was just trying to get him some money, you know, spending money, just—didn't want anyone to know about it,"

"But— he wouldn't've been able to get the money—they're not allowed out,"

"Ah, exceptions can be made," Gottfried pulled a face.

"So, you—" So, he had gone against protocol, despite staunchly defending it during Norman's last visit?

"Yeah," Gottfried nodded ruefully.

Norman grinned. "No, no, I like that. So—why a train station though?"

"Oh, I didn't want the rest of the family to know; they would've stolen it from him,"

"I thought you said they did care about him, in their own way,"

"Oh sure, yes, in their own way; but they're greedy, nasty little vipers, always grubbing, claim I owe alimony, or child support; God knows what. You wouldn't be able to find it again, would you? The ticket? It's not too much money but it's a fair amount; I could use it,"

"Ah, well, you know, I live right nearby there, you want me to collect it for you? Whatever's in the locker? I can bring it back by, or drop you there? I've got friends on the police force, they can bypass all the red tape of proving it's your stuff in there or whatnot, if I put in a good word,"

"Oh no no that's okay, wouldn't want you to go to any trouble,"

"No no, no trouble,"

"No it's fine," Gottfried nodded his peculiar, rueful and alert jab of his jowls downward.

"Are you sure?"

"Yes, yes."

"Well, let me know if you do have difficulties,"

"It'll be fine; thank you."

"I—know getting that ticket made Rene's day; he was telling me all about it. If there was one thing that did make him happy—"

"I'm so glad."

Norman hoped they parted friends.

CHAPTER 9

Still, the idea Gottfried had sent Rene the luggage ticket troubled Norman, along with the offhand way he had mentioned despising being asked to pay child support. Should he tell Wilhelm, Norman wondered, about the ticket? Had this in some way contributed to Rene's suicide, even though it had legitimately been sent by an uncle?

Norman tried to convince himself he was just being nosey. But something didn't add up.

He couldn't be sure he'd sufficiently interviewed Gottfried, but he got the impression, at least, that Gottfried hadn't been attempting to move his nephew to a more comfortable mental health facility. He was, at least, seemingly under the impression Rene really was dead.

So, there went any chances to explain away Rene's look-alike as Rene himself, shuffled through the psychiatric systems' programs in an attempt to vouchsafe him greater comforts than were available to patients in secure units like Servways. Unless this was all the grumpy Wilhelm's doing, and he hadn't bothered to tell his brother their nephew was still very much alive. That seemed unlikely.

But if Gottfried believed Rene dead, then who was the double? Not a half-brother, according to Gottfried.

Norman hadn't considered the possibility a patient could be lost within the psychiatric system due to machinations that weren't purposeful. A human error, perhaps? That resulted in two elderly men being told their nephew was deceased?

Could the hospital be padding out their numbers to accrue more funding?

But that led Norman back to silly attempts at explaining away the fact Rene's scar had disappeared. He felt like it would be adopting the paranoia patients displayed, were he to actually think some kind of ploy in that regard was at work. But what else explained the scar away? A sudden, potent regime of aloe and Vitamin E?

And if they had moved Rene, what was he doing in rehab? Surely Rene would have told him, if some bureaucratic kerfuffle was afoot; his medications had always worked well enough in the past to ensure he could express himself and understand his surroundings.

Why hadn't he recognized Norman?

Of course, it wasn't uncommon for very bad cases of schizoaffective disorder to wind up distrusting the volunteers they previously favored; in fact, the more a patient showed a preference for Norman, the more he had come to expect they would eventually drop him, cold turkey. Could eating the ticket have somehow been a release of anger more properly, for whatever reason, directed at Norman himself?

Or, suppose, Norman had simply seen a man who looked remarkably similar to Rene? These things happened.

This other patient could be suffering from schizoaffective disorder. Many admitted to the Freemont-Lowell Residential units were. Perhaps he was simply in the rehabilitation unit under a dual diagnosis, aiding recovery from substance abuse as a step prior to dealing with further mental health disorders. Eating the ticket Norman proffered could then have been an entirely meaningless reaction, a random act of insanity.

But that man moved like Rene did; he combed his hair like Rene.

If Rene had been cloned—hypothetical questions made Norman smile softly as he headed back out of Robencresent— would the clone part it's hair on the same side and use the same amount of hair gel?

The only route home Norman knew took him back by roads near Wilhelm Monado's house.

Alright, he was just going to dare himself to drive by, once more. Maybe he could gather up enough courage to overlook his own nosiness and try asking the old man if he could think of someone—anyone—in the extended family who might be mistaken for Rene. And be housed in Freemont's residential psychiatric program. He could also mention the ticket.

Norman was just passing back by the outlet to Lamhurst Drive (it was a one-way street; he'd have to track back round three left turns through the adjoining neighborhoods) when he noticed a commotion out of the corner of his eye. He braked mid-intersection, reversed, to crane his neck and peer.

Wilhelm Monado was being forcibly removed from his home by two orderlies in blue scrubs. He was putting up quite a fight. Norman put his Megane in drive again and sped to the rescue, only to realize he had no business doing so. Wilhelm's in-home assistant must have called. Had Norman triggered some sort of attack? My God that would be three individuals whose mental health he'd destroyed in one week—or was Wilhelm the one who had sent Rene the ticket, and Norman the inadvertent tipoff? –No. But something wasn't right. Wilhelm may have been privately hurting at the death of his nephew, but he hadn't seemed close to a mental breakdown, at least not to Norman's admittedly unprofessional eye. So, what the hell was going on?

The orderlies loaded Wilhelm into an unmarked van and moved on down the street.

Norman weaved back out from where he'd parked curbside to follow.

He kept at a distance, used to tracking suspects, checking his rearview occasionally to make sure he himself wasn't being followed.

The van merged onto the ramp leading down to a highway. Norman followed. 40 miles later it changed lanes to exit. This was the path Norman would be taking to return home anyway. They took exit 109. That was the exit towards Freemont-Lowell. Norman tensed.

He was right. They meandered through the side-streets he had taken earlier that week to visit Frances, until they pulled up to a white, vertically retractable fence around the back of the Freemont-Lowell Center. The gate raised. The van drove through. Wilhelm was trapped inside.

CHAPTER 10

You know, if Norman didn't know better, he'd say Frances was 100% dead on accurate, and there was some kind of conspiracy going on in that Freemont-Lowell place. He even recognized the silhouette of the unit towards which the van had pulled—once the gate was lowered back down to the ground— as that of the rehabilitation unit across the quad from Frances' residential ward; the brutalist streak of acute angles imposed a now presciently ominous shadow across the quickly fading sunset.

He watched by the fender lights of the van as Wilhelm Monado was taken inside. Why would a lapse in mental health lead to a rehabilitation clinic? Had his visit bothered Wilhelm so badly he'd taken some drug? Surely that'd lead to the ER first, even if an overdose. Besides, Wilhelm seemed like the least likely person to do such a thing; he'd been grumbling like a bigoted teetotaler when Norman left him.

Norman reversed to get out of the back-alley down which he'd followed the van, hoping, though he tried to tell himself everything was perfectly above board, that no security cameras would pick up his license-plate's number.

He pulled into the parking lot of a cafe, now closed, and shut off his car engine to give himself time to review:

One uncle gets carted off to a mental institution. One uncle claims to have sent a ticket—multiple tickets, Norman supposed, if Gottfried had also been the one to send the ticket that'd caused the fight that sent Rene to Servways—multiple tickets for a luggage locker, to his nephew in a high security detention unit that he claims he was just a ploy to smuggle the boy some spending money.

Even though he'd have to pull a fair number of strings to even let Rene out of the building for the day to retrieve the money from the locker in the first place—which reminded Norman: that was another potential oddity of Frances' story: *was* it just a coincidence she'd specifically mentioned Hugh Cossimer as being associated with whatever was going on in Freemont's rehab unit? Even at the time, Norman had known Rene getting in the car with Cossimer was against protocol. They didn't—they weren't supposed to let patients from high security units out, not even for the weekend.

Oh, it was probably all just a coincidence.

Rene's aunt's husband's brother's brother….

Were Norman still a policeman, and such discrepancies presented themselves, he'd feel he was on the trail of something, and keep on doggedly. That had won him many a case against criminals other officers hadn't even begun to suspect.

For twenty-one years, he'd found drug cartels, insurance scams, and the occasional embezzling case.

Maybe he was just bored with retirement, jumped at patterns that weren't actually there.

An odd thing: how did Gottfried Monado expect to get back in the locker at WestEnd without a ticket?

Norman's more sensible mind supposed he could simply describe what was in the locker, to prove he'd been the one to put it there. Right…. Norman was getting too old for this. But…

I'm just gonna snoop, the remnants of a stubborn little policeman at the back of his mind decided. He put the Megane in reverse and slipped back silently along the roads to Wilhelm Monado's house. If Monado had had some sort of breakdown, there might be signs of a lash out still strewn about the interior of his house. Maybe Norman would just peer in, just try to retrace, a little bit, the man's last movements, before he was dragged away. Maybe he'd gone to retrieve something out of a drawer. Maybe little old men who lived in quiet villages seldom left all their doors locked overnight. The in-house assistant might've locked up the front door and gone home or accompanied her charge to the hospital. But that left a lot of friendly-looking patio windows Norman had noticed when he'd popped round before. Casing private property came second nature as a policeman. Always some entryway unprotected by an alarm system, or some perch over a garage by which criminals could easily access second-story windows.

He'd just—you know—claim to be a friendly neighbor, dropping by. See if he could find anything that might help Monado. Wanted to make sure everything was locked up properly; he'd heard Wilhelm had to go to the hospital for a few days. Honestly, being old, Norman could get away with practically anything; it was almost worrying how automatically people trusted him, for looking slightly like their grandfathers.

He turned back down Lamhurst, driving slowly to give himself time to change his mind, if he wanted to. Any moment now.

Frances was the one who suffered from delusions. Sneaking back to Wilhelm's house was probably just straight up certifiable.

But Norman just wanted—you know, just to take a look—

Luckily, Norman was spared any more worry over his own sanity by the fact Gottfried seemed to have beat him to it, when it came to casing Wilhelm's house—or, rather—from where Norman pulled up—it looked a bit more like Gottfried was just flat-out ransacking the place.

The front door stood open. Three men were searching through papers inside. [

Gottfried stood on the lawn, making one last pawing search through cardboard boxes that had apparently been taken out of the garage, shifted through, and subsequently discarded.

"Hey!" Norman leaned out of his car window, happily. "I thought I recognized you!"

He'd decided subtlety called for his 'stupid-cop' routine. Perfected while on the beat, this routine aimed at seeming as open as possible, while remaining closely guarded. "Can I help?" he got out of his car all friendly, offering no explanation of what he had been doing driving by at this time of night. "Going over all his old papers eh?"

"Whose?"

Gottfried did not appreciate the intrusion.

"Rene's,"

Gottfried gave Norman a strange look. He had assumed, if Norman knew Wilhelm's name, he would know Wilhelm's address as well. Surely the irritatingly omnipresent volunteer visitor had found information about both brothers using the same procedures—and Rene didn't know enough about his uncles to be able to tell Norman where Gottfried lived.

"Yeah, I figured I should get started going through…" he baited Norman, to continue talking, then waited.

"Oh, here, let me help," Norman instead went eagerly to transport one of the boxes Gottfried's helpers left at the front door, to settle it more closely among the rest of the boxes out by the curb.

51

"—No, it's quite alright, we'll handle it ourselves," Gottfried took the box from him. "Thank you though," he meant it to be dismissive. But Norman kept pressing.

"Are you looking for some of the luggage tickets he was always claiming you sent him?" Norman grinned, appropriately compassionate, to imply he assumed Gottfried was simply looking for mementoes. "I can help you—"

"No no, no you know what? Just, no— we're fine; I'd, like to go over this on my own—"

"Ooh, it's so much though, I can—"

"Look, what are you trying to do?" Gottfried was sick of playing this game. "You think Rene's on to some kind of mass conspiracy? Is that what this is? You need to reflect and relax, alright? You know? I've seen your type of patient before; they get out, they think they can blend in; they think people won't notice their paranoia. Well I tell you what; it's rude, you understand? I want to be left alone."

"No no I just—I was actually just coming back this way to get to your house; I was going to explain—I used to be on the police force, I've still got quite a lot of connections there, so I could cut through the red tape myself, you know, when it came to getting that locker free— since it was my own damn fault I lost that ticket, I can try to help out; I just feel bad; I know it was a momento, eh, I dunno, for what it's worth."

It was the only excuse Norman could think of. Oddly, the weakness of his excuse served a purpose: he wanted to egg Gottfried on a little bit, just to see where he went with it, how the conversation played out—an old policeman's trick, maybe, though Norman had a sinking feeling this might only result in a conversation showing he'd gotten too involved, allowing boredom in retirement to turn him into a weirdo.

"No no, *I'll* get it, please— the locker's fine. This is— just a family matter. I understand you knew Rene, but. Try, to have a little sensibility and leave me alone in my grief! Alright?"

It was curt enough that, in order to keep playing dumb, Norman was forced to retreat.

"Of course, so sorry; I understand; call me if you need anything, I'll just—leave my card—"

"That's quite alright! Thank you!"

"Alright—" Norman stopped fumbling for his wallet, "have a good night then—"

Why didn't Gottfried want the police to help cut red tape and get the contents of his rented locker to him faster? Was he really that private of a person, to forgo convenience? It was possible.

Of course, Gottfried was right: Norman did feel like he himself was playing with fire, seeing patterns he couldn't interpret because he himself was looking in as an outsider. An impertinence? Maybe.

But the sudden, suspicious meanness.... Just what was in that luggage locker? Did Norman trust his own sensibilities enough?

Yeah, no something strange was going on here. Wilhelm....

Of course, if he tried to go through official channels in an attempt to satisfy his own curiosity—if he really did call on old acquaintances in the police department, just to see what was in that damned locker—Gottfried had every right to block him with bureaucracy and privacy rights, every chance he got.

Norman just wanted a peek, though... his hackles were raised now.

Luckily, from his policing days, he also remembered the simple truth that left-luggage lockers in railway stations are remarkably easy to break into. At least, if one has the right friends.

CHAPTER 11

Penalties for illegal forced entry weren't exactly conducive to striking up a friendship with the men Norman had met over the years who possessed this unique skill. But there had always been moments of passing recognition, especially in the smaller towns Norman's patrol covered, upon seeing the men he'd put away, now returned from their time behind bars. Occasionally, he would make eye contact with an ex-convict at the superstore or run into a particularly lippy newspaper-stand attendant, only to realize hours afterwards where he'd seen the man's face before.

One of the repeat offenders Norman had to deal with was a man named Demetry Mendel. He had never been sentenced for habitual breaking and entry; he was too clever for that, variating his methods and the timing between heists enough, though he was caught by various counties, that they could never put him away behind bars for too long.

It had become a running joke in Norman's life that were he to cross past the public gardens by Lamhurst in Glover around 6 pm, he would find almost invariably Mendel playing a game of chess or boules with other men who smelled of gin, in amongst the park benches.

Today was no different. It was pétanque tonight, as the twilight gathered. Norman could hear the soft murmur and thunk of the balls as he approached.

"Demetry?" he called out in the darkness.

"—What?" Demetry looked up to see the silhouette of an oncoming cop. "Oh Christ." He swerved out and away from his compatriots, coming closer. "What is it? I haven't been patrolled appropriately this time? Look, look at this," he rolled up a dirty pant leg to show the ankle monitor that bulged, half visible, out of his dusty sock. "It's on; it's working—"

"No no, that's fine; I'm not working; I'm retired."

"Oh." Demetry settled back down into twirling a spare bocce ball in one hand, looking Norman over. "So what do you want?"

"I need your help with something,"

"You want me to do some ratting out for you?"

"No, not quite; can we take a walk? Somewhere more private?"

"Yeah, alright," Demetry flung the ball back with a careless thunk and a call: "I'll be back!" then lit up a cigarette and followed Norman. "So, what do you need?"

"One second," Norman gestured. He bent down and signaled for Demetry to roll up his pant leg again. He took out a penlight and shined it over the surface of the ankle monitor. This was an old device, cracked with use, and produced by Tier-Guard. It wasn't a model that would have audio-recording capacities.

Demetry knew instantly what he was looking for.

"You're in some sort of trouble?"

"Maybe," Norman straightened back up again. "I've been volunteering, visiting prisoners in high security psychiatric facilities—"

"Oh no I wouldn't know any—"

"One of my friends, an inmate, recently went missing. They say he's dead. I saw him in a rehabilitation facility just 30 minutes away from the high security unit he used to live in. At least, I think I may have. I just find it odd, that's all."

Demetry grew silent, watching him.

"My friend always said his uncle had sent him a ticket that would open a particular locker at the WestEnd train station. I always thought this was just a delusion, because according to the system it was impossible for his uncle to have done so. Then, after his death, I found the ticket. Now, the ticket was taken from me. But I want to see what's inside that locker."

"O-oh," dawning realization seemed to brighten Demetry's mood and mental acumen more than pétanque had in many a day. In truth, he had been feeling the nihilism of encroaching desires for suicide lately; it was why he so readily came to Norman's intimidating beckon, without fuss. Now, the thought of an ironic adventure appealed to his better sensibilities, as a story worth enabling the telling of. "I see, I see. So, the cop comes to me—because I know what I am doing— when he finally realizes he wants to break down the walls of society."

"No, I want you to break into a locker for me,"

"Mm. Can do, for money. And a guarantee if I go down for it, you come with me, because otherwise, you know, the entrapment—it's illegal,"

"Of course; I'll be there with you. We'll break in together." If there was money involved, Norman didn't trust Demetry enough to let him gain access to it alone.

"Okay; how much do you pay me?"

"Mm. How much do these things usually cost? I think I have about 100 euros from my last pension paycheck I could afford to give you,"

"…deal. But only because this should be fun, working with a cop, yeah? And you're sure you're retired?"

"I wouldn't have to come to you if I wasn't,"

"Mm, yes I see. You miss having search warrants? Alright, you know, I might actually believe you on that one. Alright. I will do it. But this is not entrappment you understand because you are coming to me with concerns as to the welfare of a prisoner that means we are protected by laws for whistleblowers; we cannot go to jail,"

"—Err, yes," assuming, of course, there was actually cause for concern to blow a whistle about.

"This is not some grand ploy is it?" Demetry noticed Norman's reserve. He ducked round the closest tree, expecting to see officers closing in.

"No; I'm just not quite sure—it could be nothing. My friend was diagnosed with schizoaffective disorder; the ticket—everything—it could just be a delusion,"

"One that you picked up from him as well? I didn't know delusions were catching,"

"They actually can be, but—I just want to be careful. I can't promise you we'll be covered by whistle-blower's regulations."

"That's alright; I'll do it anyway. For my buddy the cop," Demetry smiled. "But you can't tell your friends—do you have colleagues, old friends? Still on the force?"

"No, no, I don't keep up with them much,"

"Then I'll let you in on a secret, how to get the locker's contents out without being seen—what's supposed to be in it?"

"Documents," according to Rene, "and—maybe—" Norman tried to break it gently, "some money; that part I'm not quite so sure about, though. He was always very interested in the possibility there was hidden money around him, but I never saw any definitive proves,"

"Alright, alright; I see. So. How much money?"

"I have no idea. Enough to make him comfortable," according to Gottfried.

"Mm alright, alright. In a card, in a little chip card? Debit card? Or cash?"

"I would think cash, if he was going to use it within the psychiatric system,"

"Alright, good, good, you see; you're thinking like me already, this is very good. Okay. And the documents?"

"Rene said they would help ensure he got the money,"

"So, bank statements? IDs?"

"I don't know,"

"Alright, so, either way: here is what we do—when do you want to do this?"

"Ah—as soon as possible,"

"And you cased the location already?"

"Yes; I've got an idea as to how we might be able to get in, as well,"

"Perfect, alright; why don't you tell me it?"

CHAPTER 12

Once Norman had explained how they could get in, Demetry felt comfortable enough to tell him the trade-secret for getting back out again.

"Alright, easy enough. The trick is, not to let the cameras see you've done anything wrong, of course. So: you straighten over the locker; you open the locker, without the camera being able to see your hands, and then—what? You are not expecting the locker's contents to be so bulky, say, or some other contingency; we don't know what will arise, but, we know no one ever brings bags to a locker they then unlock, unless it's small shopping bags from the day out, inconsequential. No, they take bags out of the locker. So, we sew into the lining of the coat we wear, a long pocket."

Ah. Norman had always wondered how Demetry managed to get away from the scene of the crime so often unobserved.

They spent the evening sewing together. It was important, Demetry explained, that all the pockets they added to their jackets should be over the chest, on the inside of the jackets' front panels. This way, they could shield from the cameras whatever it was they were packing away into the pockets, by subtly pulling the chest of their jackets to one side— in case the contents of the locker themselves should arouse a CCTV attendant's suspicions.

But it wasn't odd enough to be immediately counted criminal, to stuff ones' jacket with odds and ends left in a locker.

They could also, hopefully, better shield their faces this way.

"They'll get a record of us going in, though; they have forward facing cameras at the entry," Norman warned. There was no way to avoid these, unless they took a hammer to some back windowpanes and risked being charged with destruction of property.

"Hm. Alright," Demetry didn't like the idea of leaving proof they'd been there. "I tell you what; in case anything happens, come here, now— what type of lockers does the luggage room have?"

"Ah, old fashion key lockers they started out as, but they added an override for an electronic ticket system, you know, you put in the ticket, it opens the locker--"

"But they still have little key holes on each of the lockers?"

"Yeah they've got that for the emergencies—just in case—"

"Mm. Weird. Okay, that makes our job easier; two-pronged approach. I'll show you how to do this— in case anything goes wrong; you can complete the job, yes? So first, you take this tension wrench—"

"Alright…" Norman learned hesitantly; his fingers were too gnarled to be truly expert at manipulating lock picks, but he managed, at length, to a standard lock using the keyhole in its back.

"Good, very good. Now, the ones at the station, may be a bit more difficult depending on if the electric system overrides the old locking system. For those, you must jimmy in from the side—" this, Demetry explained, was known as an 'emergency lock override' and may require them to take off the metal faceplate that concealed the fancy new system electronically sealing the luggage lockers. But at the end of the day, inserting a key— even if said 'key' was in fact only composed of a lock pick and a tension wrench— would still be required. "So, now, you can finish the job, if you really want to. You can keep the kit," Demetry handed it over.

"Oh no that's alright I—"

"I'd like both of us to be carrying incriminating evidence,"

Demetry had been through the legal system a number of times. He knew the importance of bargaining chips. And an ex-cop who had turned to lock-picking wouldn't look good for the Glover police force at all. Demetry might be able to walk free, should anything go wrong, on the strength alone of the fact that he knew Norman had entered a luggage locker with lock-picking equipment and plausible intent.

"Alright. Well, hopefully, everything will go smoothly."

Norman had proposed they wait until night, a sentiment with which Demetry entirely agreed.

Nighttime meant sleepier attendants. Especially in a regional train station, where little through-traffic promised minimal excitement.

The West End train station, though small, was at least large enough to be considered slightly more important than the average regional hub. It had a long galley of fast food restaurants, clothing stores, and bookstores attached to the atrium past which one could gain access to the rail tracks. At night, these had all been closed, but for one or two of the restaurants.

Under dinghy fluorescents, Demetry and Norman passed by the last open fast food restaurant, closed camera shops, and the coin operated turn-styles that would enable one to enter the pristine, marble confines of a bank of showers, open for rent, receiving two rental towels as well, all for the price of 2.97€.

The entryway to the locker rooms was beside the rental showers.

Heightened security over the years had required these lockers to be encased in glass. One couldn't get in without first subjecting any baggage or coats to the interior of an x-ray machine. Demetry came first, compliantly stepping through the metal detector beside the xray machine. His lockpicks he hid in his wallet; they could pass as keys, but to save time, wallets were habitually excluded from the screening process anyway. He made eye contact with the sole attendant on the other side of the x-ray's read out and nodded.

The jacket he passed through the x-ray machine showed nothing unusual in its make-up.

About five minutes later Norman showed up.

They relied on timing their entries to seem unrelated, so that the cameras at the front of the glass casement round the locker rooms wouldn't pick up an ex-cop and an ex-con presumably traveling together.

Norman had budgeted in the five-minute window by which he delayed his own arrival by considering how long it usually took him to find a luggage ticket in one of his own coat pockets, once he had redonned all his clothes after passing through metal detectors. Added to this, Demetry could also stall, until Norman arrived to partake in aiding the accomplishment of their crime, by fumbling with the change machine set to one side of the luggage room's interior.

Demetry headed over to this red and grey machine now, and began feeding it a 10 euro note, waiting for coins to trickle out of its side. He would not, of course, be using the coins to retrieve whatever was in Rene's locker. But the jangle in his pockets, were he to collect enough of them, could hardly be construed as suspicious.

Norman was just re-donning his jacket by the time the change machine in the wall had finally given Demetry a proper amount of loose cash.

"Demetry?" Norman pretended to see him for the first time. Ensuring their gestures and body language looked natural would be of the utmost importance for tricking the cameras.

"Norman? Fancy seeing you here. You know that little son of a bitch," –he meant the change machine— "in there gave me all 20 cent pieces? 10 euros worth! Little bastard," Norman needn't have worried their lock picking would take longer than the average time it took a patron to slip coins down the slot by a locker, not if the average patron had to deal with paying using twenty cent pieces, to gradually accrue a cash balance at least equal to ten euros for each hour they'd left their luggage in the locker. Norman usually brought his own change in convenient fifty cent pieces precisely to avoid having to deal with the wall-mounted change machine altogether, but the existence of that systemic inconvenience would actually work in their favor now.

Demetry turned down the corridor to the long-term luggage lockers, a step ahead of Norman.

"Did you case this place?"

"Yeah, I came here every Sunday for about the last five years of my life,"

"Yeah? Well they've added a new security camera," Demetry nodded subtly, not daring to point. Norman couldn't turn; he could only pivot and side eye the long glass panel adjacent the long-term lockers. Sure enough, the blink of a red recording light could be seen through the tinted window.

"Shit,"

"So now what? You're staying with me while I open my own locker, without opening one of your own?" Demetry thought he could sense a sting operation, some form of entrapment

"Of course; why not? Catching up for old times' sake; we can make that stick; they haven't got anything on us, I'll stand between it and you," Norman scratched his neck casually and lent against the locker that stood adjacent number 264. He could always say befriending Demetry was part of Servway's visitor volunteer outreach program.

"Yes, but now we can't dismantle the locker," to get to the manual override, deep inside. The camera would notice two men shifting sheets of metal around.

"Can you override the central electronic monitor in any other way? Could we just pay, even if we don't have a ticket?"

"Mm. Could be…"

Demetry slipped a knife between the side of locker 264's door and the column of metal that housed the automated payment system that was meant to receive customer's tickets. They were in luck. He could feel his knife slide the thin metal plate covering the locker's coin slot back towards the center of the locker's door, enabling payment to be pushed down the slot by bypassing the computer that required a ticket in order to push the coin slot's plate out of the way.

"So, if we put coins in, we can just pay and it'll open?"

"Yes, but hurry!"

"No wait, wait; straighten up; I saw a sign that said 50's the maximum charge." That's how much they'd probably end up having to pay. "I'll get more change and pay you back for the twenty. We'll say you didn't have enough to cover the fee; it cost more than you thought it would; come on,"

"Mmm…" Demetry accompanied Norman back to the change machine, grumbling.

"Ok…"

Ten minutes to wait, while coins collected in the dish of the change machine. Demetry was getting on edge.

"Ok, ok, we try again now."

Norman took up his stand once more between locker 264 and the watching surveillance camera, making sure he left enough room it simply looked like Demetry was having problems getting the automated payment system to take his ticket.

In actuality, he was jimmying open the coinslot again.

"Ok, here's hoping."

As idly as possible, Norman began depositing twenty cent pieces, as though he were a perfectly ordinary bloke just helping out a friend, while the friend stood by watching— as though Demetry was not, in fact, sweating bullets from having to maintain constant pressure to keep the coin slot open. One twenty cent piece. A second twenty cent piece.

"Do you know how many we'll have to put in?"

"I'm assuming 50 euros worth,"

"Jesus," that was a lot of 20 cent pieces.

A digitized screen beside the locker's coin slot began counting how much they'd paid: 60 cents. 80.

"I think it'll look suspicious if I just lean here for too long—" but after having only paid two euros, the lock clunked open. The digitized screen ran astericks across its face to show entry had been successful.

"How long was this locker rented for?"

"Stuff should've been in there for at least a week by now,"

"Could they have rigged the system?"

"I don't know,"

Norman sure hoped he had remembered the locker number correctly.

Two euros' worth of luggage storage usually meant whoever had utilized the locker had only left less than an hour ago.

There was no money inside. Only a stack of papers. That relieved Norman. Documents. Rene had been right, then. No average person left nothing but a manilla folder in a luggage leave—right?

The two men knew better than to show any interest in the contents of what was meant to look like a casual retrieval.

They were lucky; the folder was easy to fold in half, before Demetry casually slipped it into his sewn-in front pocket. Both men were relieved. That would save them some explanation, were the video of them together from the back corner of this hallway ever to surface inconveniently. Norman had taken nothing from Demetry's supposed locker.

"Alright,"

As per their prearranged agreement, Norman didn't cover his tracks by now pretending to put luggage of his own in a locker. Had he done so, this would have provided him with a plausible deniability Demetry himself wouldn't have the luxury of falling back on.

They walked out of the luggage leave together, still chatting casually for the sake of the cameras. Locker 264 was left open, ready for its next user. Demetry was a pro. Not even a scratch mark had been left behind.

"Alright," once they had walked two blocks away from the train station and could be sure no exterior cameras would pick up their movements, Demetry handed Norman the folder they'd taken from the locker.

"What is it?"

"Come on," Norman motioned for them to turn down a side street, so they could lean against the brick siding of a jeweler's store and be sure the wind wouldn't whip away any of the loose papers within the folder.

Norman fumbled it open. It contained admittance forms to the High Security Unit at Servway's, for a man named Robert Espinose, who appeared to have gotten in a tussle at his last psychiatric facility over other patients refuting his claims that an influential uncle on the facility's board of directors had sent him the ticket to a luggage locker. In WestEnd train station. Locker 236.

"What the—"

Norman turned the paperwork over to find a picture. It was Rene, only he didn't have a scar running alongside his left eye.

"So, what's that mean?" Demetry was looking over one shoulder.

"He told me he got that scar in the struggle that led him to be admitted to the High Security Unit. This struggle."

"Mm, yes," Demetry could read the circumstances of 'Robert Espinose''s admittance to Servways over Norman's shoulder. "So, this has to be the paperwork that got Rene—my friend— admitted to the High Security Unit. But it's the wrong name, and there's no scar,"

"Used a different name just to fuck with you. Took the picture from documents they'd drawn up on him before the fight."

"The picture's dated the same day as the form, though," 3 years prior to when Rene first arrived at Servway's.

"Well then he was lying about how he got the scar. You said yourself they don't tell you what the patients are in for; patient tells you, they're bound to get a few things wrong; maybe he was there for longer than he wanted to let you know,"

But Wade had said Rene hadn't been in the High Security Unit long enough to get any mail. Wade had been under the impression Rene hadn't been in Servways for any great length of time too. Of course, Norman couldn't be sure when Wade had been hired. Maybe Rene had been admitted to the high security unit twice, once as Robert Espinose, before Wade's time.

"Or maybe one of them's the clone," Norman shuffled through the rest of the paperwork, irritated. He'd told Demetry about Frances' claims.

"Ah, that is your most likely bet," Demetry joked.

But Norman was still preoccupied. "Why would he lie about how he got a scar?"

"I can think of lots of reasons; he doesn't want you knowing he gets in fights while in the Secure Unit; he wants to sound more exciting—he probably got it slipping in the bathroom,"

That did sound like a possibility.

"This says he was admitted three *years* prior to when he claimed, though. Why would—?"

"Mm. It's craziness. It runs in the family, from what you said, no?"

"It's possible…."

Norman had also told Demetry about the run-in he'd had with Wilhelm Monado being forcibly removed to Freemont-Lowell.

"Or, your friend stole this guy's story, of why he was admitted,"

"But there really was a ticket for Rene, like he always claimed, amongst his stuff; and his uncle didn't deny he'd sent him one,"

"Alright, so? You don't need to be sane to recognize a luggage ticket,"

"So why send a—to anyone—to begin with?"

"To fuck with his nephew. Or nephews, I don't know," Demetry was getting confused.

"But then why bother leaving this in the locker?"

"It helps him get money, you said."

"Right. So, then I'm guessing that implies Robert is actually Rene, under a different name, and the documents somehow pertain to Rene, a false identity? But—why?"

Espinose. Was that a legitimate relative of the father of whom Rene believed himself to be a bastard? Did Gottfried just straight up lie about no look-alikes in the family? And then... send both this Robert and Rene separate tickets? Norman supposed bastards could be a sensitive topic, despite Gottfried's professed enlightened attitude about the subject.

There was another admission form beneath the one that admitted Robert to Servways. "The 7-6 Project. What is that?"

"Clones?" Demetry gave Norman a sarcastic side-eye.

"Why leave this in a locker for your nephew? And then claim you put money?"

"Because he's crazy,"

So, Gottfried was crazy too now?

"Right. But what—?" Norman flipped back through the papers.

"I tell you, you start talking too long with them it gets catching, you know; trust me. I had a sister-in-law who tried to set me up for a pyramid scheme once. They start making sense about halfway through; it's how they get you on their side, they wear you down,"

"Hmm oh I don't know. What hospital is this from?" Admittance to Servways had been signed by members of 'Wesley Crown Hospital for Psychiatric Services'.

"That's the hospital Rene came from,"

"So, it's just Rene with a different name."

They did cater to patients' requests to choose their own nicknames. But that didn't go so far as to allow for a different surname.

"Or it's two different men who aren't related but look identical."

Admittance to the 7-6 Project had been signed by psychiatrists from Freemont-Lowell....

"Why would you do this to yourself?" Demetry was actually enjoying watching Norman suffer over his own confusion.

"I know I saw..." well, he supposed— "I guess the man I saw at Freemont-Lowell could have been this Robert," that would explain the use of the nickname 'Rooky', perhaps. Espinose simply had a nickname Norman didn't recognize as Rene's because Robert Espinose wasn't Rene.

Just what the hell was his file doing in a luggage locker at WestEnd?

And why would he eat Rene's ticket, and why did he have an incident report identical to Rene's? —or, as Demetry had suggested, identical to the incident report Rene claimed to have. Maybe Rene simply had been lying, using Robert's story instead of his own. But then how had he found out about the story behind Robert's admittance to Servways? That was supposed to be strictly confidential, unless Robert himself told Rene—or Rene witnessed the struggle—but even then, to know Robert eventually landed in Servways.... Had it been the topic of a nice family chat? If Robert was part of the family of which Rene claimed himself a bastard, that was the same family that by their own admission—or at least, by Gottfried's admission—habitually avoided visiting Rene.

Perhaps, if Norman could find some prior connection between Robert and Rene—if, indeed, they were separate entities, perhaps then he would understand why Robert's folder was waiting for Rene at a train station, as, apparently, a means to ensure Rene received money. That promise alone felt to Norman like an assurance of foul play, that Robert's folder somehow brought to light—a promise to gain money by suing Servways, perhaps? Norman pocketed the folder, folding it over and placing it in the right breast pocket he had sewn down the length of his jacket's interior.

Now, to figure out what to do next.

CHAPTER 13

For this round, in the idle game of pensioner vs. state psychiatric facilities, Norman decided he needed the help of his old acquaintances at the police department, but Demetry could still be of some help too.

Despite the ankle monitor's limiting effects on his caprices, Demetry still maintained a radio dialed in to pick up chatter from policemens' squad cars, on the kitchen table of the dinghy apartment he reluctantly allowed Norman to enter.

"Up at about 212 I-9 and twelfth," came through the radio. Then: "I've got a man here says he's at a cousin's house—"

"10-47 request permission—"

"You're not supposed to be on those frequencies,"

Demetry simply shrugged.

Norman sat by the radio and started playing with its dials. "Have you heard anything interesting recently?"

"What do you mean?"

"Armed break-ins? Fugitive sightings?"

"Your buddies don't still complain to you about work problems?"

Norman had been the last of his 'buddies' to retire. But even so, all police work was confidential; they wouldn't have been able to talk about it with him anyway.

"Hm. Well," Demetry tried to remember. "There was—I think a break-in, the other night, but it might also have been a hit and run,"

"No, that won't work," –not dangerous enough. They sat listening for a while.

"10-38 may be requested suspect Patterson—"

"Patterson—what's that?"

"Oh, he was in the paper too, though—shot up a hotel lobby trying to get away with the till's cash,"

"And he's still at large?"

"They say he's difficult to track for some reason,"

"Do you have the paper?"

"I might have left it out," Demetry went to search as Norman tried to zero back in on the sound of the dispatchers, now warbling through Demetry's receiver.

Demetry returned with the newspaper.

"Richard Patterson, still wanted in connected with a non-lethal shooting last Saturday—"

"Last Saturday?"

"See? I told you, this guy's good,"

It didn't usually take the police that long to hunt someone down. Not where Norman and Demetry lived. It was too small; village life was too transparent to hide a running convict long.

"Yes, alright; Patterson could work,"

"What are you going to do?"

"I'm going to ask if my old boss can do me a favor,"

"To try to find the clones?"

"Yeah, to try to find the clones,"

Demetry had been compensated 200 euros for his services at the luggage leave, but the file on Espinose hadn't been the sort of thing he'd been expecting to find in that locker. It was enough to arouse his curiosity. "You'll keep me informed, whatever happens?"

"You bet."

The answers to whatever was going on between the nearly identical Rene and Robert would undoubtedly be found at Wesley Crown Hospital. They had both been admitted to the High Security Unit at Servways from there. But Norman no longer had the authority he needed to ask hospitals to turn over confidential patient documentation. For that, he needed a warrant, and a valid reason for wishing to visit the Psychiatric Center.

Luckily, valid reasons were easy enough to manufacture.

He arrived at the office his old boss had moved into the next morning, around nine o'clock.

Rita Sanis had climbed to division head at Norman's old department about five years before union stipulations required Norman to drop slowly out of active service and into the boredom he now found as a pensioner.

She was small, sharp, and brutish, but intelligently so, and she smoked when she thought no one was looking.

If Norman had thought it would be hard to sweet-talk Gottfried into giving up information, convincing Rita to lend him a hand would be even more difficult.

"Hey, boss? I got a—"

"Saw you with Demetry Mendel the other night," she was smoking in her office, but Norman was technically on a social call, being retired, so she didn't mind him witnessing.

"—yeah, that's what I wanted to talk to you about," *Shit.* Where had she seen them together? "He—uh, tipped me off about this fellow named Avin Patterson?"

"Oh?"

"Apparently, he's got a job running opiates from a nearby hospital." Norman's accusations against Patterson, of course, once found false, wouldn't stick to the guy's record unfairly. "I read in the papers he's on the run. Figured running opiates could be how he keeps out of custody so efficiently; he must be using it to finance himself, stay mobile,"

"Alright," Rita looked like she could like this angle.

Her department had very few leads on Patterson. Norman had asked around— just casually interested— before he entered her office. Confidentiality about police matters was still in place, of course, but an old, friendly face still learned a few things. Norman could only hope he could supply fabricated details about Patterson's nonexistent drug smuggling that were vague enough they didn't accidentally contradict something Rita's team had already discovered about the fugitive.

Also, now that he'd side-stepped explaining what he'd been doing with a known safe breaker, he needed to find a subtle way to imply Demetry wasn't affiliated in any way with this Patterson fellow. Wouldn't do to land him in the soup after he'd done Norman a good turn.

"So. What Demetry heard—from a friend who works at this hospital—is that Patterson's got an associate on the inside, locked away in the place   it's a psych ward—for depression or something. Anyway, he supplies the opiates, every Wednesday."

"He breaks into the dispensary?"

"Or—something, I mean it's not exact, but it's good information; Demetry says his friend's on the level; he's worried about losing his job, just— doesn't want this Patterson to know he brought in police, you know,"

"Mm. And the contents of the locker you were seen breaking into? What was in there?"

"Locker?" *What locker?* Norman tried to play innocent.

"You were seen breaking into a locker at WestEnd Station, 4:00 a.m., just two nights ago,"

—Two nights ago, because, to Norman's chagrin, he knew he needed a night in between the caper and returning to his old precinct, to make sure he was rested for the upcoming ruse he meant to employ. He was getting old. But being honest with himself about his own limitations was paying off now. He was alert enough to counter quickly:

"There wasn't anything in the locker; can't bust a guy for stealing nothing,"

"Damage to public property?"

"It wasn't damaged; he said he'd lost his ticket; he opened it; wasn't anything in it, so I figured I'd let him go. But, the fact I was there, is the reason, I guarantee, why I've got such good information now. He didn't know I've retired, see,"

"And he just walked right out of there, after his first attempt failed?"

"I mean what else was he supposed to do? He didn't know I was retired; I walked out with him. Figured I'd give him a second chance. We had a bit of a talk afterwards."

"Alright," Rita stamped out her cigarette. She supposed that tallied with what little she knew of Norman's movements from the CCTV cameras that evening. She wasn't concerned enough to double check if he returned to collect his own bags later. She trusted him. He'd been a good cop.

"So, will you let me track the lead he gave? I don't want to waste police time, but I could check it out myself. Please? Just for old times' sake,"

"I'm not stopping you." There was no law that said retired inspectors couldn't play private detective.

"I need help."

"Oh." *That* kind of help. Search warrants. So that's what he was hoping to gain, by coming back here to be chummy at 9:00 a.m. by the coffee machine with what few old colleagues still remembered him. "Norman—"

"No, now listen; I've got a description of the guy and I know what hospital he works out of; I just need to get a name,"

"The guy?"

"The opiates guy; the guy who supplies Patterson with opiates," it'd been a few years since Norman had needed to make an official presentation to superior officers; he was getting a bit ahead of himself. But his lie seemed to be holding up pretty well.

"Alright," Rita's eyebrows seemed to say, 'keep talking….'

"All I've gotta do is ask if they've got anyone at the hospital, filing under the description Demetry gave; I just ah—need someone with a badge to make it look official."

"Where does he work out of? The opiates guy?"

"Wesley Crown Hospital for Psychiatric Services,"

"Hunh." The name seemed to strike Rita as something of interest.

"And what's his description?"

"Got violent enough to be sent to a High Security Unit for three weeks,"

"Well Jesus; that could be anybody!"

Three weeks was the minimum standard evaluators could request when filling out paperwork to get a patient transferred. Any time Espinose spent at Servways after those three weeks would require new paperwork. That paperwork, if it existed, hadn't been in the folder.

"They've only got a population of fifty men up at Servways. Chances two of 'em came from the same psych ward'd be pretty slim," Usually, they came through the prison system.

"Oh, that's right; you do that—reading with the—"

"Visitor Volunteer and Listen Program, yeah,"

"Alright. I'll lend you out a sergeant," and a search warrant. "I hope you're on to something; this guy's been leading us on wild goose chases for about a month now!"

Well, Norman thought, then surely one more wild goose chase wouldn't hurt,   right?

CHAPTER 14

That night, Frances couldn't sleep.

She'd gotten a new neighbor, very early that morning, around 3:00 a.m.

Hadn't seen him yet; he'd stayed in his room; that was one of the perks of being allowed your own key.

He hadn't come out for dinner. She hadn't seen anyone new come to line up at the dispensary for night-time medications, either.

She'd gone back to her room after that and sat with her ear to the wall on the side of the room from which she'd heard orderlies introduce her new neighbor to his new facilities, the night before.

Being admitted at 3:00 a.m. in and of itself wasn't necessarily odd.

Orderlies ran all sorts of tests on you when you first arrived at Freemont, checked your blood pressure, and reviewed your medications with you. That entire process could last late into the night, if you'd been transferred in as something of an emergency—Frances supposed. At any rate, if patients misbehaved, they had to wait in holding cells till doctors could see them to calm them down, so maybe that'd happened.

No, what struck Frances as odd was not coming out of his room to eat at all. That was odd.

Frances had struggled with anorexia over fears of malevolent poisoning. An orderling had followed her around for three months—before she'd realized it wasn't poison they were using to keep an eye on her—it was the birds.

The orderly had assigned her a point system from 1 to 10, scored daily, based on whether or not she achieved her goals of eating satisfactorily. And if she got less than 8 she was sent to talk to a special psychiatrist who tried to reason with her and increased her medication dosages.

There had been no orderly outside her new neighbor's room, to see why he wasn't eating.

Now she listened, quietly, scrunched against the wall.

"Frances? What are you doing?"

Damn; she should have closed the door.

"I was just resting my head,"

"Alright; you want to watch Cavalcade? They're showing it in the commons room,"

"No, no,"

"Alright,"

That was the good thing about people thinking you were insane. You never had to justify yourself. You could just say no and leave it at that. No politeness required. No subtlety.

She could hear a faint breathing and grumbling on the other side of the wall, a strange, lilting accent when her new neighbor talked to himself, like he was cutting off the ends of words by swallowing them.

'Must be foreign or lower class,' she thought to herself. Maybe that's why he wasn't eating. Some sort of religion.

She heard the familiar clanking of orderlies' keys that night around 4:00 a.m. Phones were ringing at the nurse's station. A gentle shushing murmur of orderlies checking up on one another from various units maintained monotony.

"Yes, we've just had a   "

"… oh, try down the hall—"

The tinkling set of keys had been inserted into the door to the room next to Frances. She rose, fully alert, darted to the wall between herself and her mysterious neighbor, and listened, heart pounding.

"Alright sir, we're all ready to transfer you over," *Aha!* 'Transfer.' – Typical. They always used that word.

"No—no no; I won't go; I don't like it—!"

"It's just routine counseling for group therapy—"

"Then fuck that! I know what this is all about that shit head—"

"Now; now, it's alright; it's alright Mr. Monado—"

"Fuck you,"

"Your brother's waiting; it's purely routine; we're not gonna do anything you don't want to—"

73

"Oh, Gottfried'll make sure everything's okay, won't he? —fucking Gottfried,"

"It's all very painless; I promise; it's just talk therapy—"

"Yeah and—weaseling—get your hands off me! Get off—!"

By now most of the patients on the floor had woken up. Most simply sat, leaden-eyed, staring at the ceiling, waiting for sleep to reclaim them, if it ever would. But a few, like Frances, stood and peered out into the corridor. They weren't allowed, for safety's sake, to unlock their doors until the orderly knocked on each at 7:00 a.m. the next morning. The safety precaution, explained every time they went over group protocols in community goal sharing sessions, had been put in place precisely for instances like this, to keep patients from endangering one another. If patients didn't obey the requirements, their key-keeping privileges were revoked.

But that wasn't why Frances didn't open her door to look closer at what was happening.

No, no; she was scared to make herself stand out, not now. She already knew this was a cloning kidnapping. That was the only thing it could be. They were going to clone that man—cockney accent and all. "It'll all be very painless" — "just a group therapy session," —that's what they always said; she'd heard them enough times to know. So, she slunk back to her bed, to sit and play innocent as she listened to the echoing twist and skud of her neighbor's footsteps, as the orderlies whose voices she never recognized trailed away with him down the hall.

CHAPTER 15

The sergeant Sanis sent to help Norman enforce his requested search warrant was a short, grubby man in his early forties who was clearly not looking forward to aiding Norman. He actually sighed when they finally pulled up at Wesley Crown Hospital for Psychiatric Services. Norman led the way, from the carpark in to the nearest information desk.

These facilities were set out almost exactly like Servway's more secure units, in that visitors were required to pass through two fail-safe checkpoints, before being admitted to the sunnier, silent side of imposing concrete walls.

The sergeant, whose name was Collin Hayes, let Norman do the talking too. Norman was hoping to find out anything he could about the time both Robert and Rene had spent at Wesley. The original paperwork documenting Rene's transfer to Servways could also help clear up whether Rene had been lying about why he'd been transferred. Norman could request it as follow up, upon receiving Espinose's documents. He just had to hope the ruse he'd set up would work.

He approached the front desk.

"Hey, I'm here with a search warrant for medical records, the state is interested in procuring information on a individual suspected of drugs trafficking," the paperwork was handed over.

"Ok, you'll need to go to our Systems Manager for this,"

The Systems Manager tried to tell Norman it was too late in the day to procure the information he sought. It was only 3:00 p.m.

"If you come back tomorrow—"

"No, it's a matter of urgency,"

Luckily, the paperwork reflected that.

"Alright…." The medical staff had been hoping to obtain legal advice before acquiescing to the search warrant's demands. The nebulous nature of asking after a patient without knowing their name seemed illegal.

"I mean, do you have anything concrete to go on…?"

"Yes," Norman directed the Systems Manager to Page 3 of the Search Warrant, detailing probable cause. "We know the man has been sent to the Secure Unit at Servways Protective Facilities for assaulting a fellow in-patient over claims his uncle sent him a luggage ticket for a left-luggage locker in WestEnd Train Station."

Collins was surprised.

He hadn't realized Norman's search had such specific criterea to match.

"Alright, this might take a while, I guess we'll need to cross-reference…"

Actually, searching medical records for patients who had been transferred to Servways took a matter of minutes.

Norman and Collin received a type out of the requested information at 6:00 p.m., at which point, all Norman's carefully spun plans went out the window anyway.

There were two men who matched the description of the drug-runner Norman claimed he sought. Rene Cartesius, who had been transferred to Servways from Wesley four and a half weeks prior, and Robert Espinose, who had been transferred under similar circumstances three years before.

Both intake forms clearly explained: the patient in question was transferred after starting a fight regarding the fact other inmates didn't believe his uncle had sent him a luggage ticket, for a locker in WestEnd Train Station.

What the—?

So, they were fudging intake forms, somehow?

Could such twinning have suggested cloning to Frances' mind, if she were picking up on a related phenomenon at Freemont-Lowell? How would she have accessed--?

"So how do we tell which is helping Patterson?" Collin no longer found Norman's methodology all that impressive.

It was a good question. –Or, it would have been.

Norman skimmed down the information available on both men.

Both were blood type O positive. Height and weight practically identical. One had significantly higher blood pressure, but that wasn't much to go on.

Had Rene simply cycled back through the system under another name? Or was this some grand conspiracy by his uncle—whichever one kept sending him tickets to train station lockers—to keep him insane? It certainly was doing a number on Norman....

"Is there any way to prove these two men aren't identical?" he asked the medical records attendant.

"Um," the attendant had thought differing names would have been enough to go on. He studied the records. "No, you're right; they do seem fairly similar,"

"Hm." To keep Collin from becoming suspicious, Norman needed to keep acting like he was trying to track an inmate purportedly smuggling opiates out of Wesley's facilities. Unfortunately— "it says here neither of these men were transferred back here, to Wesley, after their time in the Secure Unit?"

"No,"

"Damn."

That meant they weren't at Wesley during the time Patterson had been on the run. The tip Norman claimed Demetry had given him didn't add up.

He had to pretend to be disappointed.

In fact, he was astonished at his good fortune. If Rene had lied about why he'd entered Servways, it was a lie official records reflected. So, either it wasn't a lie at all, or someone was tampering.

His search for the nonexistent drug runner at Wesley, though, had come to an end.

The hospital's records as to where his so-called suspects were located now stopped with their transfer to Servways.

"Not bad though," Collins left relatively pleased. "We have the names now; we should be able to find them—or him, if you're right and it's the same person twice. We can at least ask if he's in any way involved; maybe he's been involved in the drug runs before and you were simply fed old information."

"Yes... I wonder though...."

Norman hoped he hadn't landed this Espinose fellow in trouble. He no longer resided at Wesley; he no longer fit the profile Norman'd told police to search for. But he knew better than to think they'd leave well enough alone.

"I'm just worried if my information source claimed the opiate smuggler was operating out of Wesley—and Espinose isn't there, and Rene isn't there— maybe we're on a false lead again,"

"Maybe that's how Patterson does it; feeds us false stories—Maybe your source of information is closer to Patterson than you realize,"

77

"Ah yes, good point…."

Norman had to walk a fine line here. He didn't want to bring suspicion down on Demetry. "Or maybe he just had the wrong facts at his disposal. Or just wanted to get me off his back,"

"That's wasting police time,"

"Not if I'm the one stupid enough to put the order through, come on."

They drove back to headquarters, to report to Sanis.

"So, you think if he's housed in a different hospital that automatically negates the lead?"

"Well, where is Patterson operating out of? I mean in general; have we managed to triangulate?"

"His robbery was at Ludgate; that's all we have; we think he may have been seen up north near Rochester, but the evidence is sketchy,"

Luckily, both Ludgate and Rochester were very much in the opposite direction from Freemont-Lowell—where Norman had last seen the man who could possibly be Robert Espinose. If this identification was true, Patterson, in his theoretical drug-runs, would be going far out of his way to transport drugs from Espinose. So, hopefully Norman could comfort himself in knowing charges against Espinose could never stick. He hadn't just set an innocent man up. He'd honestly thought they'd find Espinose was some alternative name for Rene, somehow. It was still possible; they simply hadn't proved it yet.

"So, should we follow up?"

"I've got nothing else to go on,"

Damn. Now Norman was the one wasting police time, for the second time that week. Should he just tell them he had located Espinose in Freemont Lowell? Did he know for sure the man he'd seen was Espinose? It would be good to have confirmation—

"I'm just worried it's a wild goose chase," he admitted, down cast. "What if I look into it on my own? No more wasting official police time,"

"We can do that; I'll contract you out as a private detective."
Norman's old degree in criminal justice qualified him to be a PI.

"I hope I'm on to something," he shook his head, relieved.

78

CHAPTER 16

Walking in to Servways with a search warrant felt like both Norman's worlds were colliding. But he told himself he was doing it for Rene. Really, this was simply going above and beyond in his duty as a visiting patients volunteer.

Staff at Servways told Norman Robert Espinose really had been transferred from Servways to Freemont-Lowell, about two years prior to Rene's arrival at Servways himself. Norman wondered if that transfer corresponded to the 7-6 Project's intake paperwork in Espinose's folder from the train station.

"Where abouts inside Freemont-Lowell was he transferred to—?"

But of course, Norman already knew, really, from what patients and orderlies told him: "stepped down" patients, who had been allowed back to units with lower levels of security were routinely housed in the residential units of whatever hospital had an opening. And indeed, that's where records showed Espinose had been house. There was no mention of the 7-6 Project.

So why would Espinose have been put in rehab subsequently? There was no mention of substance abuse on either of the confidential medical records Norman had seen. He asked Wade as he was leaving. "Are there ever patients who come here with substance abuse problems that aren't caught? Who then have to go to the rehab unit after they've already been admitted?"

"Well, usually the withdrawal symptoms are pretty obvious,"

"And if they were getting drugs from the inside?"

Maybe he had inadvertently stumbled upon a set up that actually did involve drug smuggling.

"Well, that would be a breach of almost every hospital regulation—"

"Yeah, I know,"

"You saying you think that's been happening?"

"No, I'm just—trying to figure something out," he didn't want to tell Wade too much.

"You're coming back to see Vincent Friday, right?"

"That's right,"

First, though, he had to keep his appointment with Frances.

It was convenient. While he was at Freemont, he could ask to see Robert Espinose in his new official capacity as PI for Glover county. He just wanted to ask a few questions, to try to see if this man was in fact Rene, just with a new identity.

Scars could be painted over, he supposed, or fake to begin with—if orderlies were bribed to pretend not to notice. And they were certainly a good way to fake the existence of two separate men, when one wanted to disappear into a new identity. Then he could see whether Rene's uncle had shifted him to a comfier facility, or if the change in identity was related to some strange drug scheme. After all, why would they keep 'Espinose' in the rehabilitation unit otherwise? He'd already been in the psychiatric facilities system for months by now; he ought to have gone through withdrawal already.

Frances, though, threw a wrench in his plans.

As soon as Norman sat down, she started right in.

"They cloned another patient while you were away,"

"Oh! But— they haven't harmed you, right?"

"Only because they knew you were coming back; someone would miss me,"

"Your sister would miss you too, I'm sure,"

"But she wouldn't be able to make the connection,"

"Have you talked to her about this? —about what you're worried about?"

"She'd tell the doctors,"

"Well, maybe that's a good idea; you haven't—done that yet? You know how we were saying—maybe you should tell the doctors?"

"No, no no Norman. Now I know you're on my side; I know you half believe me 'cause you didn't tell the doctors either, or they would have come for me by now, upped my doses,"

It was true, he hadn't told Freemont's psychiatrists about her delusions. He felt guilty. He never liked to pressure patients into making admissions they didn't feel comfortable with, but it would be to Frances' benefit to be completely honest about what she was afraid of… wouldn't it?

He sighed.

"What have you been up to?" She meant it as an attempt to understand why he hadn't betrayed her trust and told the doctors about her claims.

"I've been trying to follow up on—" he paused. "The patient I went to see in the rehabilitation center last time I was here,"

"Rehab?"

"The... cloning—?"

"Oh, yeah yeah; Egbert's friend?"

"Right." Close enough. "It is just a rehab center— you know, for— drugs," hopefully that knowledge would enable Frances to feel at least slightly less nervous.

"Tallies with what I've heard."

"What do you mean?"

"Well that's what they always tell patients when they come to take them away; they're taking them to therapy,"

"That's not necessarily rehab—"

"Eh, the way they kick up a scuffle it is,"

"So, you think they may simply be in need of—substance abuse assistance?" *Was this all drug related?*

"No, no, that's just what they say to them, to get them to come along,"

"Right. —And you say another patient was taken in the same way? Recently?"

"At 4:00 a.m. On the dot. Just this Monday."

She had no way of knowing it had been 4:00 a.m. She didn't have a watch. But she would bet a great deal of money, had she bothered to look at the clock on the wall by the nurse's station, like she had many times before, that 4:00 a.m. had been the time she'd been woken.

"Who was he— the patient they took? What was he like?"

"I never saw him; he never came out of his room. They just keep 'em here as a holding station in between sometimes, I suppose—at least, that's what I'm starting to think anyway,"

"In between what?"

"In between units,"

"Ah. Why here, in particular?"

"Because we're close to the cloning—the rehabilitation unit,"

"Right." Shifting vocabulary was making it difficult for Norman to distinguish how much of Frances' delusion had grasped her mind today, and how strongly it had done so.

"So, the patient who left Monday; he was here for a week? Or, for how long?"

"Only a day, and a night; they took him out after that; he didn't even come out for dinner,"

Could this simply have been an auditory hallucination? Norman knew Frances did suffer from them.

"He had a funny accent too: 'I won't go I don't like it,'" she put on a full cockney accent. "I think he might have been foreign; they called him Mr. Monado."

Norman blanched.

"Whu—did they say what he was in for?"

"Group therapy sessions with his brother,"

"At the—rehabilitation unit?"

"At the cloning, yeah; they're gonna clone him; don't you think? "Brother," "clone" it's all a code. I'm telling you; I've been in this unit long enough, I know,"

"But you've never seen one of the clones,"

"I've never seen 'em together, but you can tell they're clones,"

"How?"

"Because they always come in pairs, you'll see; there'll be another Mr. Monado in a few weeks' time, only they won't call him Mr. Monado, but he'll sound exactly the same—and if he comes out, which they usually do, for food or to be weighed or something; he'll look exactly alike, only he won't be being called Mr. Monado and they'll say he's a new patient just trying to fit in; that's what happened last time, fellow you saw, through the fence, fellow you were looking at, who ate your paper,"

"The—he came back through here twice?"

"Sure. Once a few years ago, then again right around the time you came snooping; only stayed a night the second time. Like I say, it's a clearing house; and they'll be after me next if you don't sign up again—"

"I will. I will sign up again; of course. Can you ask to be transferred if you're feeling uncomfortable?"

"Not on your life; too much fun,"

Frances grinned.

She enjoyed this delusion. She'd be bored otherwise.

A horrific stumbling block, but Norman supposed it was better than the alternative of suffering horribly from the illusions her mind produced.

"But are you frightened?"

"Not with the safeguards in place. You're a safeguard. You know,"

"Do you have other safeguards?"

"I've got a new one; that Hugh Cossimer actor; you've seen him, in ManHunt? He comes round, sometimes,"

"I know; he comes to Servways too,"

"Yeah well that's where I heard of him first; you can rent him out, you know. A friend of mine at Servways did. Anyway he's in the volunteer system, so I've finally gotten signed up to meet him. I told the nurse I needed someone else, on the outside, someone they can't make disappear. I'm seen with him and then I disappear, people are bound to ask questions. They scrutinize the famous that way."

"I thought last time you said he was in on the cloning,"

"Oh, everyone's in on the cloning,"

"But this time, he agreed to meet with you?"

"Yeah. Oh of course, because I intimated, I hinted to the nurse, that you know, I knew what was going on, so she put me on that list,"

"Frances…. If we're going by the logic of what you're telling me, and assuming the cloning is true, that doesn't sound safe at all—does it?"

"Well, depending on who you trust. I've got it all worked out. I'll splash a drink all over him, so the paparazzi take a picture; then, I'll have my picture in the paper, and I'll be noticed. Then, people will ask, 'whatever happened to that lady who was out with Hugh Cossimer that day?' They might even check up on me. So then, I've got a double-blind security going on; they can't get at me, because I'll be too well known."

"Well, I'm—glad you get to meet Hugh Cossimer,"

"I know; I know; I've been trying for months, but oop—just drop a hint about the clones—I got that from you, I figured, if you thought I was on to something, I must be on to something, so oop—just a hint about clones, and they scheduled me right in, right away,"

"Frances…." No, could he do it? Further her delusion still more? An obligation to foster sanity vied with his own temptation to veer into believing a conspiracy he knew had to be half mad. But still, the fear presented itself that the last time he had seen Rene Cartesius, he had been getting in a car with Hugh Cossimer.

But that was insane. Demetry was right; he'd simply been listening to madness for too long. Cossimer wouldn't hurt Frances.

He kept quiet. He needed to think. But Frances was very talkative today. She'd been bored lately and appreciated the distraction.

"I've even been eating more recently, so he'll take me out for a celebratory milkshake,"

Norman grinned. "I'm so glad to hear that. Tell me, Mr. Monado— which direction did they take him—to the right, or—" as he had last time, he pointed first in the direction of the door at the far end of the hallway, then towards the door that would lead out from the corridor of patients' rooms to the cafeteria.

"Same as always," Frances pointed towards the cafeteria.

But that would be—towards the rehabilitation center.

Suddenly Norman wasn't as interested in interviewing Espinose as he had been upon arrival. He wanted to find out what had happened to Wilhelm Monado.

CHAPTER 17

Norman returned to Sanis the very same day. Only Sanis didn't have time to see him. A Deputy Chief had been assigned to oversee his movements instead.

"I need another search warrant. For medical records, pertaining to Dr. Wilhelm Monado."

Was he starting to believe his own conspiracy theories? What had started out as an excuse to use the old police systems he had become accustomed to was starting to turn in his mind into a justified hypothesis. Perhaps drugs were involved, if whatever operations Frances was picking up on were taking place within the rehabilitation unit.

The search warrant was processed in about 3 hours, no questions asked.

"You think you're on to something then?"

"Yeah,"

"You might need this,"

They deputized him for extra legal protection.

Norman went back to Freemont the next day, to request access to all files pertaining to Wilhelm Monado. He brought with him the folder of documents he'd retrieved from the luggage locker at WestEnd. Perhaps Monado would have something to say about it.

"No, I'm sorry; we don't have anyone by that name staying here with us at the moment; I'll see if we ever—"

"Was he discharged recently?"

The nurse clicked through her files. "Mm, no sir, I haven't got anyone in my files with that name for the last eight months," that was how far the easily accessible admission files went back.

Another mystery, then: smuggled in, flying under the radar, undocumented in official channels— just like Rene's luggage ticket.

"Alright."

It was too much of a coincidence that Frances' hallucinations should pronounce the name of a man Norman had only recently seen dragged into Freemont involuntarily.

Moreover, the delay between when Frances claimed her neighbor had been taken away, and when Norman had seen Monado first admitted, suggested Frances may have been right: her unit could be some sort of in-between storage area, for those on their way between one unit and another.

Norman went back to his car to get the notepad he traditionally brought to take notes on what patients said. He needed to review this— whatever might be going on—with Frances. On second thought, he'd show her the files on Robert Espinose he'd retrieved from the luggage locker in WestEnd as well. Maybe she'd have something to say about them.

Then, he decided, after he had accumulated as much information from her as possible, he'd confront Espinose himself. Was this man really Rene under a new identity?

His eyes latched on to the sight of Demetry's spare lock-picking kit, in the backseat. Almost on instinct, he tucked it in the front of his jacket. He was still wearing the contraption he and Demetry had sewn together, doctored unnoticeably to be able to carry three times the normal amount in its pockets. He needed all the help he could get, if they were denying Wilhelm Monado had ever been to Freemont hospital before. He'd seen the man enter!

He arrived at the residential unit, unannounced. "Hi, I'd like to speak with Frances Hayworth, please? It's very important,"

"Frances is in Community Forum right now I'm afraid you'll have to wait,"

Norman waited.

"You wanted to see me?" Frances pottered over.

"Yes,"

He waited until they were alone in the conference room again.

"Ok, now, try to tell me as much as possible what the process is you think is happening with that cloning. It takes place in the rehabilitation unit?"

"No, no, below it, in the basement. But, you know, they house there. I guess, but you know, it's all connected."

"Right. Ok. So, the basement— how do you know that?"

86

"Because the lights are on down there sometimes, as late as 10pm. They say it's a special therapy group. And they always say it's a special therapy group when they come for people to clone, yeah? You don't need to be a genius to put two and two together,"

Oh no. Of course, there were going to be multiple different types of special therapy ongoing simultaneously in a psychiatric hospital. Norman didn't give up, though.

"When did they tell you those lights were a special therapy group?"

"You mean what—? Uh… around 10:30pm, I guess; they took one of the patients once when we were milling around for our socializing hour; we have an hour to watch movies after evening medications and she was there,"

"They came for her then?"

"Yeah, for the special therapy,"

"I thought you said you never got to interact—really—with anyone taken to the—cloning, special therapy?"

"Usually I don't—but you're right, with this one, I did,"

"What was she like? You got a good look at her?" Norman flipped through his notes. "Do you know who she was? Where she'd transferred from by any chance?"

Frances grew very quiet.

"Frances?"

"She looked like me,"

"How much like you?"

"Enough. She was only here for a day. They let us hang out by ourselves. Then I screamed at them til they took her away."

"You never saw her again?"

"No,"

"And did anyone else see you two together?"

"No; they put us in our own little conference room for a while, just so we could talk, get to know each other. She liked plants,"

Sounded pretty boring. Aside from suspicions of cloning.

"And was there anyone—"

"Oh yeah, sure, there was an orderly part of the time; I mean I'm sure they were always watching us,"

"And do you know why they let you two stay off together? In your own room? Some sort of special privilege? What did they say?"

"They just said they thought we'd like one another. It was like they were testing us out."

"And she looked like you?"

"Yeah, I thought so."

"Ok, thank you. I'll—probably be right back," he still had to ask her if anything about Espinose's paperwork rang any bells—fitted into any of the patterns she might have noticed. But first— he slipped out of the conference room with nothing but a hurried, preoccupied nod. He'd never heard of sequestering two patients off to one side before, just to make friends—

"Excuse me?" Norman returned to the orderly at the entry to the residential unit. "Can you explain a certain phenomenon one of my conversation volunteers has mentioned?" They always tried to refer to patients participating in the conversational programs as volunteers themselves. After all, one didn't *have* to participate.

Frances came to spy from the conference room's door. She'd never seen Norman so perfunctory. Even when she'd been housed at Servways, retirement had already erased policing from his habits. Now, the authoritative attitude had returned in full.

"Do you ever pair people off together, who seem like they might be a good match? Is there ever any sort of buddy system on this floor? Maybe, during one of the social hours?"

"Yeah sure, all the time; especially if someone's not feeling well that day, we might pair them with an orderly—"

"No, this was a patient-patient pairing— in their own conference room?"

"Eh, that can happen; we generally try to have everyone stick together in the commons-room, of course, but, yeah, I suppose; you know, sit in your own corners, read—"

"Alright, thank you. Can you tell me, Frances Hayworth's schizoaffective disorder. Does it include visual hallucinations, as well as audio?"

"A-ah…" the orderly didn't know whether he should view Norman as a visiting volunteer or a deputy. Did that information require a search warrant?

"Just—off the record; I already recieved Frances' answer, I just want confirmation before I base requesting a search warrant on the testimonial of a witness whose delusions may motivate her to bare false witness to her own disabilities,"

"Ah. It's—usually just audio. Is that what she told you?"

"No visual hallucinations recently?"

"Uh, none that have been marked enough she's complained about them,"

"This would have been um, anytime within the last three months, I guess—or ever, at all, while she's been here,"

88

"There have been times when her delusions were acting up where she has reported visual symptoms, yes,"

"Alright, thank you."

Hopefully that was all this unknown doppelganger had been, an innocuous patient colored identical to Frances by her own psyche.

But Norman wanted to be sure, now. Psychedelics could produce a similar affect. If administered without patients knowing they had been drugged, resulting visual hallucinations could be marked down as within the parameters of the patients' disorder. He'd suspected this place of padding suicide rates before now for better funding; that sort of data manipulation was common enough—even well-meaning, as long as it didn't cover up a bona-fide murder, or disappearance. Could someone have been slipping psychedelics—?

"I'd also like access to the basement levels for the unit across the way," he'd been escorted in to see Frances by an orderly before; he expected, as a deputy, someone would be available to escort him over to the basement he wanted to inspect.

"Which—?"

"The rehabilitation unit,"

"Oh, I'm sorry sir those basements are off limits for reasons of structural security,"

"Structural security? Can you explain a bit what that means?"

"Ah, there are no exits to existing carparks, so we refrain from allowing public admittance as it could be a fire hazard."

Great. That meant Norman really did have to go get another search warrant, if he wanted to see the rehab basement.

CHAPTER 18

Norman was just exiting to return report to his old department headquarters, after promising he'd return to ask Frances more questions tomorrow, when he saw Hugh Cossimer himself walking through the front doors to Freemont-Lowell.

"Mr. Cossimer, I'll just check your ID," a man whose job matched that of Bently back at Servways was scanning the laminated plastic square all visiting volunteers always brought along with them.

Norman paused, indecision guarding him from acting.

Cossimer couldn't be here for Frances already, could he? Norman waited for the actor to receive the all clear, then followed at a distance. Sure enough, Cossimer was headed to the right residential unit—Frances' floor.

"Oh, I'm so glad to meet you Mr. Cossimer," he could hear Frances' aged voice from beside the reception desk, through the swinging doors Cossimer had just pushed through, to enter her unit.

Shit.

Suspecting Cossimer wasn't just idle, was it? He was the last person Rene had been seen with. If anything about Rene's death did prove irregular, Cossimer might be a chief suspect. What should Norman—?

"Well, I was thinking we could go out for an ice cream…."

Norman drew back into an intersecting hallway, to watch as Cossimer signed Frances out from the unit and departed with her towards the elevators downstairs.

He watched the elevator's descent as it was illustrated by the circles above the shaft's steel exterior door. The circle representing the floor below them turned red. Then the circle representing the floor below that. Norman realized he was holding his breath. The elevator had gone down past the first floor, which led out to the lobby, and straight to the residential unit's basement.

He pressed the down arrow of the elevator to his right.

There was no access to the outside from those basements— he had literally just been told that. So, they weren't going out for ice cream.

Course, that could've just been a bureaucratic runaround. Maybe there was some sort of way out through the basement—to avoid paparazzi. Norman tried to untense his shoulders as he stepped into the elevator that arrived for him. Down to the basement he went.

He could tell instantly why they didn't want the public down here.

The basements were barely anything but pipes and live wires. Was this really an alternative method Cossimer used to make it towards the car park? And that fancy Bugatti Veyron? Seemed unlikely.

But did Norman really believe Cossimer's arrival suspiciously sudden? Surely Frances would've been more excited if she'd known he was coming so soon—but then again, with so many patients to visit, Cossimer probably could never afford to be too exact about predicting when precisely he'd get around to meeting volunteers. It could be nothing. Or, Norman thought idly to himself as he walked forward, someone could have disliked the fact Frances had finally admitted to Norman she believed she herself had been cloned. That did seem like one of the patterns she'd claimed Freemont-Lowell didn't want outsiders noticing, didn't it? Of course, that would mean the conference rooms for patients' visitors were bugged. No one else could've heard what he and Frances said otherwise. They weren't supposed to bug the conference rooms, if that was actually a thing that was happening. That was against patient confidentiality agreements. Norman was finding all sorts of malpractice, if any of his worries actually matched what was going on in reality.

The basement's floor rose slowly up a sharp incline, ridged to help slow run-away linen trolleys, and painted dark blue.

Norman found himself exiting its cramped confines into a cool, tiled hallway, identical to the hallways that housed interior operations for the rest of Freemont-Lowell. He peered around as many corners in the corridor as he could, past as many intersecting hallways, to try to find any sign that could tell him where he had arrived.

Finally: 'Rehabilitation Center: B Floor. Staff only.' The door marked 'staff only,' Norman realized, was the door he needed to walk through.

He could hear muffled talking, a shuffle, keys. Where had Frances gone? Where would Cossimer take her?

"Excuse me sir? I'm afraid you can't be in this part of the building,"

"I'm with the Glover police; I've been specially detached to come here; I'm looking for my friend Frances Hayworth; she was just seen moments ago entering this section of the building, and I'm trying to figure out where she might have gone,"

There had been no alternative path one might have taken through the part of the baesment that had been overhung with pipes. Cossimer and Frances would undoubtedly have come out here, into these hallways. But then—where would they have gone next? "Now, I need you to assist me in locating this woman; her name is Frances Hayworth,"

"I'm sorry sir but we don't allow members of the public down in this section of the hospital for reasons of patient privacy—"

"I have a search warrant that circumvents that privacy; if you refuse to help, we can haul you in for obstructing the police." He showed the orderly his badge.

"I'm sorry sir, but members of the public aren't allowed down here,"

"What? I just showed you—"

"If you'd come with me please sir,"

"No," Norman pulled his arm away, "you're not allowed to lay hands on a working officer—"

"Sir you need to come with me." The orderly gripped him by both arms, pulled strongly.

"What the—" Norman heaved back, arching his shoulders in to collapse into dead weight suddenly enough the orderly couldn't hold him.

The man gripped him by his waist instead now, twisting his wrist to one side, "I'm sorry sir but members of the public—"

Norman shoved him in the ribs with one elbow.

They were the only two down here. There were no cameras. Norman scurried frantically towards the nearest intersecting hallway, hoping to find someone. But the orderly was faster.

In a flash he had his arm round Norman's neck, pulling him back from the adjacent corridor's line of sight.

"No—now—" Norman huffed, hair askew, panting, stomping down with both feet in an attempt to flatten the toes of his assailant. "Ai— aight!" He hollered in lieu of saying 'enough,' smashing back his free right arm to connect with the side of the orderly's face, taking advantage of the momentarily pull away this caused to grab the orderly's hair and ram his head sideways into the wall. Then he punched him hard, in the chin. The orderly fell, unconscious.

CHAPTER 19

Now Norman was frightened by his own tenacity. He had to press forward now—but how? In a moment of clarity, he jangled aside the orderly's coat pocket and grabbed the link of intertwined keys at his belt, tugging the lot off with one uncoupling of the clump's main carabiner, and rushing off, his own stout panting accompanying the jangle of his new acquisition.

He had guessed correctly that the doors labelled 'staff only' would be locked; he could only imagine this must be where Frances and Cossimer had gone, if they managed to disappear so quickly. His own elevator hadn't been that far behind theirs.

Now he had 23 keys to try in that lock. He wasted no time. The orderly would be waking soon. Norman's left-hook wasn't nearly as powerful as it used to be.

The first ten keys didn't work. The eleventh psyched him out for one hopeful moment, but ultimately didn't work either. The twentieth key opened the door.

Norman slipped in, instantly locking the double metal doors closed again behind him and noting that the key which had worked had 'A76' engraved on its head.

He thought he had known silence before. The courtyard at Servways, never quite inhabited by living creatures, which couldn't get past the walled security. But the hallway in which he found himself now was truly silent. Only the whirring of an air conditioner's compressor 2 stories above accented the absolute absence of animation.

A single row of glass block windows lined the top of the wall to Norman's right, all the way down the hallway. It was dark now, but they would have provided adequate lighting during the day. From outside them, he could hear the flutter and scoop of pigeons perching. Norman heard a coo and saw the warbled outline of a bird through the glass. He eyed it, drawing closer. Was it watching—?

'No no, no no no, no way, calm down; okay, I'm going crazy,' he laughed at himself, shaking off the feeling he was being observed, to continue down the corridor.

This ended in a second locked door. Norman repeated the procedure of trying every single key, making a note of the different engravings on each head, searching for one akin to 'A76.'

But the key that eventually opened this door had only the maker's trademark stamped into its head: 'Swize.'

Norman slipped through, adjusting the bundle of keys so that he kept the ones marked 'Swize' and 'A79' firmly in his grasp, in case he needed to make a quick escape. There had been no sounds, yet, of anyone running after him. They hadn't even turned on an alarm. That might be protocol when working in a building filled with naturally nervous patients, but Norman had been present many times when alarms had to sound at Servways to bring orderlies running for a particularly distressed resident. Could the absence of alarms mean whoever ran Freemont didn't want others to know the rehabilitation unit's basement was there to be broken into? Or—had the orderly simply not been found yet? Norman knew he'd hit him in a way that guaranteed his safe recovery, but just how deserted was this section of the asylum?

He now appeared to be in some sort of atrium. Office doors lined the far wall; a hallway lay open to his left. He read the labels by each door. 'Dr. Jack Velmortin, Lead Geneticist.'

Norman knew enough about history to feel automatically uneasy at the thought of a geneticist and psychiatric wards working together. What was in that office? He looked down at his set of keys. But this door, it turned out, when he tried the handle, wasn't even locked.

He snuck in. The filing cabinets, of course, were all securely bolted. Only a new patient's intake form lay out on the desk. Norman felt for the lock picking kit Demetry had provided.

Did he dare? Search warrants and deputizing wouldn't cover this.

Of course, he dared. Something felt wrong enough to frighten one of his patients; he volunteered to make sure the patients he was assigned to felt safe.

A soft memory of the radicalism that governed Demetry's modus operandi flashed through his mind as he slipped the tension wrench and pick from Demetry's lock picking kit into the nearest cabinet's top-most drawer's lock. It opened with a 'chink.' Inside, the folders were heavy, laden with paperwork; he pulled the nearest few out to lay across the desk. 'Harven, J.R.,' 'Nabiscen, L.D.'—these were patient files.

He risked turning on the desk's lamp.

These first few documents appeared to be standard release forms. Norman flipped through until he reached a table of numbers that looked promising.

It appeared to be a list of abnormalities in the genome of Harven, J.R.. 'Irregular T Cell' was the only vocabulary on the page Norman recognized; the rest were conglomerations of Latin prefixes.

He came next to a diagram of a man.

Did Nabiscen's file contain the same—? It did.

Maybe Norman would have more luck trying to translate the legal vocabulary on the standard release forms at the beginning of each folder.

"I hereby consent to a duplication via somatic cell transfer of all unique memories and algorithms by which my neurological pathways connect—"

No.

It couldn't be—

Norman dug Espinose's folder out of his pocket. They were the same intake forms. The 7-6 Project. The third document in Espinose's file contained the same pages as the first pages of the form on Velmortin's desk. They just didn't include the final contractual obligations. Just a list of height and blood pressure....

Who were the forms on the desk for? Norman flipped to the last page, where a patient would sign. Just blank—they hadn't been signed yet.

Norman went back to scrambling through the three folders on Espinose, Harven, and Nabiscen.

"...and hereby handover all legal rights to the duplicated individual at the hour of their complete regeneration to become a separate entity according to all legal jurisdictions..."

Norman flipped the document over to its first page again. "I, Harven J.R.—" the name had been printed into the document, not filled out by the patient.

He retraced his dance round the desk to the unsigned intake form he'd cast aside, and found the paragraph corresponding to that he'd just found in Harven's— "I, Frances Hayworth..."

His blood ran cold. Frances hadn't wanted a clone. And yet here were the documents, all ready for her to sign. He turned back to the back pages of Harven's contract, and Nabiscen's. Did those signatures look legitimate? Done under duress? Drugged? Harven's looked like it shook.

Why was Espinose's folder lacking the contractual agreement Harven and Nabiscen shared? It was supposed to come after the preliminary physical's results.

Norman dug through the filing cabinet he had jimmied open in search of files pertaining to Espinose. But the cabinet's last demarcation only read 'August 2054.' They hadn't alphabetized the cabinet's contents. A security precaution?

He ran through Espinose's physical again, the intake forms for the Secure Servways Units, anything for a date—2053. Alright. To the left, then?

He jimmied open a second drawer.

The folder Espinose's file came in didn't match those encompassing Harven's paperwork, or Nabiscen's…. Perhaps whoever'd left the paperwork for Rene had supplied one of their own.

But Norman had guessed right; this cabinet went back to 2052. Must have been hard to duplicate a person; only about eight folders existed per year.

Espinose!

There it was!

Most of the paperwork, including the list of unusual genes, was still in place. But not the first pages of the release form. Those Norman held now, in the clump of papers he'd found at WestEnd. It seemed someone had taken only part of Espinose's documentation— To ensure no one noticed anything had gone missing? As for the rest of Espinose's paperwork that had remained behind in Velmortin's office, it seemed Espinose had signed a contract too—barely a scrawl. Norman tried to scan it quickly; it seemed different than the legalize he'd read before— just a different format? Could doctors drug a patient into submission with drugs fine-tuned enough they could then sign documents involuntarily? Or could some threat be involved—forced use of further psychoactive compounds? Norman didn't bother reading through the rest of Espinose's contract. He'd do that later; he needed to continue snooping.

He put the rest of Espinose's bulky file in his coat pocket, replacing Harven's and Nabiscen's files in the hopes that the absence of Espinose's, being dated earlier, as it was, would go unnoticed.

These cabinets appeared to be the automatically locking type. Norman slipped the two filing cabinets he'd searched back into an almost locked position, but kept them open, compromising between the need to avoid detection, should someone pass through, and the wish to be able to come back to double check specifics without wasting too much time, should he need to.

Where did the other doors in this atrium lead?

The next office was labelled 'Identity Tracking Administration.' Its door was locked.

Norman took a deep breath and started in again with Demetry's lock-pickers. He scratched the door handle. He hadn't realized how stressful picking a lock could be.

But he managed to get inside.

A desk-top card-catalogue for keeping contact's business cards looked promising for collecting information.

Norman flipped through the cards: Navore Census Bureau, Alcanine Census Bureau—these were all the Census Bureau locations per county. 'Internal Affairs Births and Deaths'....

Seemed Norman would have to jimmy open these filing cabinets too, to find out more. He hadn't heard a sound since he'd been down here. The place appeared deserted.

Five minutes of feverish fumbling in the dark, and again, he had his first cabinet open, drawer trundling out to display further patient files.

'Manova, C.Q.'—any file would do. Norman took the third from the front, to lay it out on the desk.

'Born Quarry Falls, Nevanam, 2032, to Basil and Ariadne Threep—'

What followed appeared to be an extremely detailed outline of a family tree. He'd have to risk turning on the desk lamp again. This had to be related to the cloning—no?

Why would they need these, though? To know the genetic disposition of the people they were copying? Did a patient's great aunt somehow provide more information about his genome that the person's actual genes?

'Internal Affairs Births and Deaths....' —Supposing the entire family tree had been fabricated, to give clones a false identity?

Norman wrote down the names, quickly, noting their relationships to one another. He could double check with the federal branch of the Census bureau— unless, of course, he realized, these people had already been fabricated, created, and inserted into the bureau's censes, to provide an origin for—he heard a slight shifting outside, as of someone dropping a paper to one side.

Oh no. He had closed the door to the Identity Tracking Administration office. Now he froze, deciding it would appear less suspicious if he kept the light on. Surely identity trackers sometimes came back to their offices unannounced?

He slipped back behind the filing cabinets, to keep their bulky silhouettes between him and the door and waited. Nothing further moved. Perhaps he had heard a ruffling of pages he hadn't noticed, in his abstraction, that he himself had been making.

He went back to snooping. It might be a good idea to make doubly sure these ancestral trees related to the geneticist's work next door.

Narven had been dated 2054—no, Harven, that was: Harven, J. R. —Did they order files by date in these cabinets as well? Yes—Norman decided he ought to just look for Espinose. 2052 or 2053; one of those years. He was in 2050 now. He bent to unlock the cabinet underneath the one he had already opened. No, these were 2049, damn. Back the other way, then, newer patients to the left.

He estimated two cabinets over might house 2052, if each cabinet held about 12 folders, and about 8 patients a year were cloned. If— indeed, this Identity Tracking office had anything to do with the geneticists next door. He couldn't help assuming they had to be interconnected.

He opened the next cabinet; it gave him some trouble; he was working too quickly, frightened now. He had to calm himself back into working efficiently. Ah, here was 2052… 2053—just a few files in the cabinet's very back, but Espinose, luckily, made the cut-off.

He opened Espinose's file out onto the desk again, trawling through a complex geneology of names that looked familiar. Dorothy Fornier had married Jebediah Monado. Jebediah Monado had a sister named Norma Monado who married Roderick Espinose, 2042. Oh shit. He hadn't bothered to track Norma any farther than to see that she existed as a sister to Jebediah, had he? What did that mean? How could Espinose be—were all these records fakes?

Or had Espinose been the one to sign the agreement to be cloned? Norman hadn't read the form Espinose had signed carefully enough— he took out Espinose's folder from where he'd folded its bulk into his pocket—dozens of—stupid—contracts, where was the one he'd seen signed—?

There was a warehouse of microfilm the federal government kept in case census records online were ever destroyed; the transfer to all records online had taken place around 2045. Maybe the microfilm records would show the original census' records, assuming the entire genealogy for Espinose had somehow been cooked up and implanted within the general population's records in 2053. It was worth a shot. Norman wrote down all the names in this genealogy as well, to keep straight precisely what this office's records claimed—

He was in the process of scribbling when he heard someone outside the door, walking across the atrium. He froze, took the risk and peeked out the door's shuttered window.

From the back, that man looked remarkably like Espinose. Walking out of a side room, from the open hallway to the atrium's left. He'd come to refill a plastic cup with water from a cooler. Now, he walked back the way he'd come.

What the—? How many Renes were there? No, don't go mad. Norman forced himself to put up the paperwork he had completed copying, again careful not to fully lock the cabinets, only giving the appearance he had done so.

Then he snuck out of the ID trackers' office and closed the door behind him soundlessly.

He slunk towards the open hallway.

He turned a corner.

There was Rene. Complete with scar. He was standing in the middle of the adjoining doorway, walking out of a side room. "Ren—" Norman stepped back half a pivot, startled.

Rene turned. "Norman?"

'My God I have gone mad,' was Norman's first thought.

Rene side-eyed the room he had just come out of, then moved toward Norman. "You're not supposed to be here?"

Norman opened his mouth for a great comeback, but then ameliorated: "I was told you'd killed yourself,"

"No, they're just holding me here for isolationed quiet therapy,"

"What—?"

Rene shrugged. Norman didn't have to finish his question: 'what is that?' It allowed him to ask his next question much faster:

"Why?"

"I don't know; I didn't do anything, but it's supposed to be soothing,"

"Are you alone down here?"

"Pretty much, day in day out. I mean there are always tons of doctors and stuff, for company and all,"

"Look; I found your ticket, the one your uncle sent; they gave me your personal effects,"

For the first time, Rene realized he ought to be more alarmed at Norman's claims Servway's administration system thought he was dead. But other curiosities were more pressing—

"Did you open the locker? #264?"

"Mm."

"You found the money?"

"No, there wasn't any money. I suppose your uncle meant you could sue? Maybe? With what's inside— There were claims or—proof—" Ah, how to put this gently? "… you may have been cloned."

"Oh, of course; I've always known that,"

Rene seemed confused as to why his uncle would even bother, "I'm the clone."

Espinose walked round the doorway to the side room Rene had recently vacated.

"Robert…." Norman had the distinct impression it was now time to leave.

"But that's not just something you tell people, you know," Rene hadn't noticed Norman take another step backwards towards the doorway he'd just come in by.

"Right…"

"It's most likely why I'm here; the brain didn't—take right,"

"Or it might simply have been the brain they copied," Robert smiled, "that bares the fault."

Alarms to alert staff a dangerous patient had escaped went off.

Rene gave Norman a funny look. "How did you—get in here?"

"Yeah—" Norman nodded, glancing round quickly, "I think those might be for me," he meant the alarms.

"Shit! What'd you do?"

"Awh, they're gonna think I did it—" Robert flew instantly into exasperated eye rolls.

"What'd you do?" Rene still pressed his friend.

"Some—orderly— tried to stop me—"

"Oh my God; you gotta get out of here,"

"How? Is there a way out that way?" Norman rushed for the door on the opposite end of the hallway Rene and Robert stood in.

"No no don't go that way!" Robert caught him in arms much stronger than the orderly's.

"Why not? I can't go back!"

"Go back into the basement; how'd you get in? Keys?"

"Lemme hide in the—"

But the only furniture in the room Rene and Robert had just vacated was a bed, bolted down to the floor, without bedding, and two bolted stools. "Shit." Norman couldn't exactly hide under the newspaper Rene had been reading.

"Go back out; they'll let you out easier if they think you didn't get in here!" Rene hissed, tugging Norman towards the doors he had come through.

"What do you mean?!" Norman knew exactly what Rene meant, but he wanted to see how willing Rene was to aid illegal cover-up measures.

"They don't want outsiders to know—"

"What'll they do to me?"

"It's still in the experimental phase; they haven't patented—"

Well, of all the things to be worried about—

"Just slip back out to the front," they shoved him through the atrium, "say you got lost and thought the orderly was trying to cart you off as a patient so you panicked—"

"But what about—Frances? Frances! Has a little woman come through her with white hair with a man named— with Hugh Cossimer? With Hugh Cossimer?"

"What, an older—?"

"Yes! Kind of—short?"

"Yeah, I saw them!"

"Where'd they go?"

"I dunno,"

"I need to find her—"

"No, you need to—"

"I need to—with Hugh Cossimer?"

"Yeah! What of it? She's on a date with a movie star! She'll be fine! Go!"

"But you were—and—" Norman ran, Rene locking the door into the atrium behind him just in time. They had both heard the clanking arrival of orderlies, into the hallway that housed Robert and Rene's isolated quiet therapy.

Norman ran back from the atrium down into the cooing, air-conditioned hallway. He fumbled for the key 'A79'—he wrenched open the door—and promptly fell into the hands of 5 orderlies on the door's opposite side, who were trying to open it just the way he had been.

"Ah—"

"Got him,"

"Sir, you're not supposed to be down here,"

"Police—official police investigation!"

"No,"

Five orderlies subdued Norman in seconds.

"I've got my badge,"

"Did you bludgeon an orderly unconscious in the B floor hallway?"

"I'm on an official investigation—"

"Did you bludgeon an orderly unconscious in that hallway right out there?"

"I panicked; I thought he was taking me away as a prisoner—inmate—!"

"Yeah; you're gonna need to come with us."

CHAPTER 20

Norman was marched away under the steady pressure of two orderlies from the Secure Unit associated with Freemont. This unit was really only a holding cell, used to house violent in-patients until they could be transferred to Servway's more trained personel, but hospital procedure also allowed the unit the use of two conference cells in the basement of the residential ward's wing. The cells were barely more than dank, concrete, symmetrical barracks, with metal tables, bolted down as per usual, in the middle of each room, with stools bolted to either side of the table.

Without sunshine to filter through the row of glass blocks that lined the top of this room's back wall as well, Norman felt they didn't even need to transfer him to a police detention unit. They had all the elements of an interrogation room right here.

"So, let me get this straight," the head of internal security came in to sit with Norman, while waiting for county police to show up. "You attacked an unarmed orderly—"

"No, the orderly laid hands on me; I thought he thought I was a patient,"

"He specifically told you not to enter the restricted area you were then later found in. And then you stole his keys?"

"Look—I was investigating—I'm a deputy—I was deputized,"

"Yeah, we know."

That made it even worse. He ought to have known better than to use unprovoked force. And he ought to have known the limits of his own search warrant.

"Ok, we're gonna put you under citizen's arrest until we can get the police from county—"

103

"I am the police!" (from Glover, though, not actually from the county in which Freemont was located— that would be Merrenden.) "Look, I'd—like to make a phone call. I need to make a phone call—please?" He called over the security head, as Merrenden's policemen entered the cell. "I'm allowed to make one call?"

"You'll make it from the station,"

"No, no I am police; you're obstructing justice. I need to make a call!" He showed them his deputy's badge.

The two policemen from county eyed one another.

"Alright, one call. Just one, buddy, okay? You can make your call." They stood on either side of him as he dialed from the nearest psychiatrist's desk. The orderlies surrounded him too. This was… slightly uncomfortable.

He called Sanis directly, bypassing the deputy chief he'd been put in contact with.

"Sanis?"

"Yes?"

"I've discovered an illegal lab under the rehabilitation unit at Freemont. It's not for drugs. It appears to be some sort of artificial cloning operation they're performing on human beings. They don't want news of it leaked; I've been arrested,"

"Cromel—?" he could tell from the groan that now came through the line she was rubbing her forehead dispassionately, "don't tell me this is what you've been doing…"

"There's an entire secret lab down here, where they house—"

"That's not a secret lab; that's the Cloning Project at Freemont; every major divisional head of municipal forces knows it exists,"

"You knew about this?"

"Yeah—we. I was actually part of a team helping run an experiment for the Cloning Research Facility earlier this week—that's when I saw that footage of you and Dewey—"

"—you mean Demetry?"

"Yeah, Demetry." Sanis didn't develop close emotional ties with ex-cons the way Norman did. "One of the clones in our county's been acting a bit odd; we tried to humor him—"

"The clo—what?!"

"Sir you're gonna need to be a little less excitable," one of the orderlies closed in, "or we're gonna have to ask you to terminate the phone call,"

"Right, right, sorry—look, I have papers that were—I need you to—"
he couldn't tell Sanis he'd tried to smuggle paperwork out of the
building. Not with security listening. "Okay. When you say clone, do you
mean like a full body, like a full person clone? Like a cloned person?"

"It's called therapeutic cloning,"

"That is not therapeutic cloning! I've researched therapeutic cloning!"
He'd been looking into therapeutic cloning to get a better kidney at one
point!

"Wha—it's an advanced stage—where are you now Cromel?"

"I'm at the—Freemont hospital; they're threatening to process me
at—Merrenden Intake— look I have papers that prove what I'm saying I
need you to take a look at them—" he tried to convey an urgency Sanis
mistook for implying this may have something to do with the Patterson
case.

"Alright. Oh jeez; you didn't tell anyone external to the facility about
this, did you?" Only the two policemen from county who were currently
listening to their phone conversation. "It's just a very sensitive patient
confidentiality process; clones don't ask to come into existence the least
we can do is make sure they're not discriminatorily maligned—"

"You just—what?"

"Sir—" one of the orderlies finally attempted to interrupt over the
phone, "I don't think you understand the gravitas of this situation; he just
physically assaulted one of our orderlies—"

"He what?"

"We've put him under citizen's arrest for unprovoked violence,"

"Norman!"

"The man was trying to forcibly detain me!" Norman tried to call
over the orderly into the phone's mouthpiece so Sanis could hear, "he
was trying to deflect my investigation!"

"You had no jurisdiction to be in the basement—"

"I have a search warrant— Sanis! This is important! I have papers—
you need to see—"

"He's guilty of aggravated assault."

"They're trying to make sure the papers don't leave the hospital—"

"Sir we're gonna have to ask you—"

"What papers? What is—?" the head of internal security was
beginning to realize he may have missed something when he searched
Norman for weapons.

"You need to hang up now sir; this is getting too heated—"

"What is—?" Sanis could only hear that mass chaos seemed to have
erupted. She checked the clock on her wall. It was already after work
hours anyway. "Alright—alright, Norman? I'm coming down there."

"What?"

"I said I'm coming down there. Just hang on. I need to talk to an orderly—" they put the nearest one on. "Just try and get him in a room without police, alright? We don't know how much he knows. And Cromel?" They handed the phone back over to Norman. "Don't say a word to anyone or I will personally make sure you never see the light of day outside a cell-block again, you understand?"

Sanis hung up with a groan. She should have never let Norman back onto a case. There was a reason union stipulations required retirement at 50. The world simply worked too fast for some of these older cops. Now she'd have to go see if she could tease any information about Richard Patterson out of him. Had that all been a ruse? Jesus. What was that idiot—?

She arrived very much not in the mood for small talk, parking beside the grass quad that had once housed the monthly fair for Freemont's residential program and meeting Norman a few minutes later within the confines of Freemont's high security conference room. The two policemen from county had been left outside to guard the door. Only two orderlies and a manager from Freemont remained now, to watch over Sanis and Norman.

"Alright, what happened?" she sat down across from him. "Let's start at the beginning,"

Norman's suspiciously doctored inner-coat pockets had by now been discovered and relieved of all their contents by the county police. A lock pick and several stolen files were now arranged out of Norman's reach on the table in front of him. Norman himself had been handcuffed to the table's side.

"Did you get any new information on Patterson? Charles" —that was the Deputy Chief— "said last he heard you were trying to find a Wilhelm Monado?"

Oh, Jesus—Norman'd entirely forgotten about Wilhelm Monado! Another case in point; another mysterious disappearance!

"Yes, now, shortly before he disappeared, either Wilhelm, or his brother Gottfried, sent a ticket for a luggage locker to their nephew Rene inside the Servways High Security Units; they bypassed the entire system—"

"And this has something to do with the opiates Patterson's running?"

Please, Rita thought to herself, *please tell me you have at least something on Patterson.*

Norman had temporarily forgotten who Patterson was. Then he remembered. "No— I don't— I don't know. It could be. I think maybe—maybe Patterson disappeared for the same reason—no—" he was getting confused in his panic at realizing his superior had been in on the conspiracy of silence surrounding cloning at Freemont. How much did he dare tell her? Would his investigations, meager as they were, be swept under the carpet?

"I just—"

"Start at the beginning." Sanis got out a notepad and paper, to see if she could make any sense out of the garbled threads Norman seemed to have pulled together.

"Alright." Norman realized he didn't quite know what the beginning was. "I suppose I was first suspicious something untoward was happening at Servway's Secure Unit facility." He'd have to tell her about the ticket again; maybe she'd get it this time. "I found one of the patients I'd been seeing had been correct when he told me his uncle had managed to smuggle him a luggage ticket, despite the fact the system never recorded the fact he'd received any mail, and orderlies aren't supposed to smuggle anything in to patients,"

"Right. It's against the Hippocratic— Continue,"

"So, I had been told this patient, Rene—" should he tell Sanis Rene's name? He stopped, deciding not to disclose Rene's last name, at least— for whatever good it might do the two of them. He no longer trusted Sanis. "I'd been told he'd—my friend—'d committed suicide. So, I went to view the body. They wouldn't let me view the body."

"No, it's usually moved from on-site mortuaries as soon as possible,"

"Right. But while I was at the facility where Servways said he—my friend—the patient, had died; I saw him—the patient on the other side of a fence, very— alive. And when I told him I'd gotten the ticket he'd been talking about he ate it."

"He—?"

"He ate it; he ate the ticket,"

"Oh, right, okay." Maybe Norman had been on to something when he suspected this was all related to drugs. Sanis made a note.

"That man, though, who I thought was my friend, turns out, is named Robert Espinose; he's not the patient I was seeing at Servways. He just looks almost exactly identical to him. And I know this, because—"

Oh no, what should he tell her?

"Because you jimmied open a locker in WestEnd Rail station and stole the folders it contained, is that right?"

How did she know what had been in the locker?

Was that the experiment she'd—? With the CCTV?

"I had to find out what was going on—"

"Yeah, okay, no," Sanis repositioned. *That one's on us*, she thought. *Oh shit.* Should she take the risk and suppose Norman knew *anything* valuable relating to the Patterson case? He seemed so damn adamant about getting her to see that paperwork—but if she trusted he knew what he was talking about, she'd have to explain what exactly she knew about what he'd found in that luggage locker. If Norman thought it pertained to Patterson…. She could only assume a promised link between the fugitive and jimmying open a locker was the only way Demetry could convince Norman to accompany him to steal folders out of a public luggage leave. Did that mean Demetry knew about this? He had told Norman about Patterson…. "Alright. This doesn't leave the room, alright? We've got a confidentiality agreement we can get you to sign; I need you to sign it before this goes any further—can you get—? Thank you," Sanis signaled for one of the orderlies to retrieve a copy of the agreement to sign.

She waited, silent, until the orderly returned.

CHAPTER 21

Norman scanned the document they put in front of him. 'Nondisclosure Agreement for Participation in The Cloning Program at—' "woah no no—no no no I'm not about—"

"Just read the document Norman. It's standard confidentiality—"

"So –what, the—what— there's—just, cloning. And everyone's okay with that?"

"Yes. It's a standard procedure. Just, we're gonna need you to sign—"

"What the--? No! What--?"

"We need a nondisclosure throttle when dealing with the program for the clones' sake. We can't further the Patterson case until you sign this so I can explain to you what's going on and we can compare notes."

"But—whu—?"

"Just sign the damn form Norman."

"Okay…" Norman signed.

"Okay, so. A while back—" Sanis paused, recalibrated, then started again. "For a long time, we've been having problems with one particular patient. He's generally well-managed—but, as he is one of the clones, I get called in to deal with it if anything goes wrong because if it's clones, they can only tell so many people cloning's involved, got it? That's how I'm involved. So, okay, this patient in particular—"

"You mean his clone?"

"No, they're—both equally considered to be patients,"

"Okay."

"This man in particular kept trying to contact a family member of the man he'd originally been cloned from—I don't—how much did you discover? They're cloned from people originally, and then, given as closely parallel lives as possible—you—right? You got all that, right? Ok. So. Well, this man, let's call him—"

"Wait wait I'm sorry—what do you mean they make their lives as parallel as possible?"

"Right. So, the donor—we call them donors—"

"You mean the original copy?"

"Right, it—'s just considered derogatory, y'know, 'original'—"

"Ok, yeah, donor; got it; sorry. So—?" It always was hard to try to explain new technologies to underlings over 50.

"It's," Sanis sighed. This was an offshoot they may not have time to go down. She didn't want to spend all night explaining peripherals, not if there was anything to be gleaned about Patterson from the nominal purpose behind Norman's investigation. But maybe that was hopeless. Maybe the old pensioner really had just completely duped her, into allowing him to run amuck in places he didn't belong.

Great. What a lovely end to a tough day at the office. She'd expected more from Norman. He'd been a good officer.

"Alright." Well, either way at this rate she'd be eating chips alone in a gas station parking lot for dinner anyway. "So, paralleling each clones' experience with that of his or her donor has to do with the therapeutic properties of twinning experience—that's what they call the—" surely Norman could figure out what that euphemized on his own, right? He looked like he was following. "Right. So, the idea, is that we often find patients find a sense of shared purpose helpful, if someone with precisely the same psychiatric uniqueness has similar experiences. This way they can talk about the same things, they come at the world from the same point of view; since it's a unique point of view, this may be the one chance they get to compare notes with someone who actually understands what they're going through, so we try to make sure their experiences are similar, to aid that process."

"Except, one was cloned into existence in a basement lab—"

"Right, well—"

"You don't tell them they were cloned?"

"Not at first. Eventually, after several therapeutic sessions—"

"What if one of the clones told the other clone they were the clone?"

"What?"

Norman was beginning to understand what might have happened with Frances. "I've got another friend, a Frances Hayworth—"

110

"Norman. Norman I'm trying to get to the bottom of how on earth you think this is all related to Patterson; if you have pertinent information please contribute otherwise let's just, try to get this ironed out so you know what you're working with, if you need the information to follow up on Demetry's claims."

Right. Best Norman keep silent about how he'd fabricated those claims of drug-smuggling in the first place, then.

"Alright so, you understand why the clone's experience parallels the donor's?"

"With the—? Right; they make the clone as close as possible to the original,"

Ok. Sanis let the epithet 'original' slide. "Yeah. Alright. So. For the— locker thing. Ok? So, this man, one of the patients who has been twinned— the problematic patient I was telling you about— let's call him C, was trying to get a message through to a resident who happened to be staying at a facility for psychiatric care, you understand—unrelated to the cloning project in any way. He wanted this inpatient to take the weekend off—which you can do—"

"Right, at the residential care facilities,"

"Right. —Get in a cab, go to WestEnd station, and get some documents, which he presumed would be enough to show this patient— who was, again, at the time, entirely unrelated to the cloning program— about the program itself; he wanted this information to get out, whether as a whistle-blower or just ornery I don't know; that was his plan, though. Luckily, his donor was high up enough in the residential psychiatric facility system where their nephew was—"

Oh no. Norman realized who they were talking about. Or rather, realized that until this point, he'd actually been fairly correct in what all he'd managed to figure out.

"The Monados—"

"You okay?"

"You're talking about the Monados?"

"Yeah," what else was Sanis supposed to be talking about? "This does not leave this room, you understand?"

"Yeah,"

That must have been what she meant by the fact clones were given as closely parallel lives to their original donor as possible! Forget how Rene and Espinose were somehow accused of the same violent tendencies—*that*, Norman realized, could be the purpose behind the Identity Tracking Administration he'd broken into. '*My aunt's husband's brother's brother…*' It always had sounded so convoluted, hadn't it? Almost as if… the relationship had been contrived. To make a second uncle for Rene…. To parallel….

"So Monado was the first?"

"The—wait, which—?"

"To be cloned; he was the first clone?"

"Yeah, well, he was among the first to take part in this new comprehensive—sort of—all-encompassing project,"

"The 7-6."

"Right. Now, he agreed to form a test subject because his nephew was at that time in residential psychiatric care; they were hoping something gleaned from the experiments might aid in the nephew's recovery—are you following me?"

"Yes,"

"Alright. So. C—Monado—was one of the first to be cloned. His new brother sent a luggage ticket to his nephew in residential psychiatric housing, requesting he go to this particular luggage leave, to find—what he said was money, but which was actually—Monado came to find out himself—"

"The —original Monado—"

"Right, Monado A, Monado #1. Monado #1 found out that Monado #2 was trying to tell his nephew about the cloning experiments at Freemont. Of course, at the time, as they are now, these experiments were top secret for patient confidentiality purposes,"

That was a fancy way of saying the doctors behind the experiments knew parliament would never stand for this, wasn't it? Norman fidgeted in his seat.

"So, had Monado #1 not discovered his brother was trying to out the program—I mean, you can imagine the results had his nephew gone to the police. Now, where I come in. Monado #1 forgave Monado #2 absolutely. You know, this is precisely the sort of thing Monado #1 himself would do; he would want to tell the world; want his nephew to know what he was up to.

"We intercepted the leak to his nephew too late, though, so now his nephew knew about the program too, he just knew not to tell anyone. Now, Monado #1—in conjunction with Monado #2—because remember a lot of the donor's memories transfer to their new brother or sister, so Monado #2 is just as qualified as a psychiatric professional— Monado #1 and #2 thought, well hey, y'know, this process has helped us grow as individuals, I think we can call it a success. And as Robert—"

"Robert?"

"Right, the nephew Robert Espinose," Sanis tapped the folder in front of Norman. "As Robert knows about the whole process now, maybe we can do this same thing for our nephew, help him come to a better understanding of himself, get him sort of outside of himself, being able to communicate with someone like him, so he doesn't feel as alone in the world, so, the nephew agreed. And so, we went about the cloning process for Robert—and—in time, another young man who went by the name of Rene Cartesius," Norman nodded along.

Rene had said he was the clone— Norman just hadn't been able to internalize it, somehow. That explained why they had to pretend he was a bastard....

"Now. Here's where this folder comes in, right?" Sanis fiddled round the edges of Robert's file again. "See, in order for the twinning experience to be effective, both siblings need to have a paralleled sense of the world around them, right? Which, you're entirely right, isn't going to happen if one brother comes into the world knowing he's a clone, right? So, the memories for each clone are temporarily reset to before the donor knew about the possibility of being cloned. Then, we provide them with similar stimulus to what the donor experienced right before learning of the cloning procedure it's a very, Norman, this has been going on for almost forty years now it's a very advanced therapy that's been proven to work—it's. Well, so, so we get the new clone in place; he's set to experience the residential psychiatric program before we bring him to interview with Monado's nephew—and he gets another ticket in the mail. We think."

"He did get another ticket in the mail. That's the ticket he ate,"

"No, that's the ticket Robert ate, you mean—and no, this is the ticket Rene got at Wesley, before he was transferred to Servways."

"Sure, right, and then he—got another ticket while he was at Servways?"

"I guess? Right? I mean, that makes sense; I suppose Monado #2 didn't want him to think he'd just hallucinated the first ticket he sent—I mean it's—as you can imagine trying to figure out what is and is not reality—it's just— Ok. So, what you have to understand is that Robert was never supposed to get that first ticket. He was never supposed to get any tickets! It's a breach in protocol. Well, so, okay, but we need to reduplicate Robert's situation with Rene.

"So, Monado #2 sends the ticket again. But, this time, he's placed different paperwork in the luggage locker he's trying to lure his nephew to; it's paperwork that proves the nephew is a clone—not just that the cloning process is going on in general, right? It's got full proof that this man is a clone—medical records—identical—everything Rene needs to take to the police for the police to at least think some horrific conspiracy is at foot—duplicating intake forms—whatever they might think. Of course, municipal heads'd be able to explain, like I'm doing now, but it gets out to too many people, it still causes panic, right?

"We were gonna be okay with reduplicating the fact Rene learns about cloning the same way Robert did; it's not great, but it seems like an important 'traction point'—as they call it—in Robert's narrative that the two brothers may like to explore together.

"Alright, so that's why we've got the camera all set up, right ready to intervene at the right time, introduce Rene—eventually—to his brother, only this time around, like I said, Monado #2 switches out the paperwork—which we only discover when we find half Espinose's original file is missing—all to tell this new nephew that he himself—ie Rene—" she barely whispered, "is a clone. Which would give him access to probably one of the most startling revelations possible right while he's in the process of being treated for identical neuroses to the disorders we are trying to cure in Monado's—nephew #1, okay? That would be no good, right? That would not be no good at all. So we have to put a stop to it—we need to know why Monado #2 keeps doing this, psyching out his nephews, while opening the program up to breaches in confidentiality—which, as you've described, seems to be exactly where you come in; he managed to get that information to you,"

"Actually, that was more my friend Frances,"

"Okay? Okay." Now Sanis had to figure out why Norman could possibly think this whole fiasco of a breach in patient and procedure confidentiality had anything to do with Patterson. "So, you think this Frances has something to do with Patterson?"

Norman realized he needed to keep up the pretense of linking Monado with Patterson, if he hoped to get any more out of Sanis.

"Maybe. Let me get this straight, you—well first off, you knew what I was doing at the locker this entire time?"

"We didn't have the manpower to go check if it was the locker 416 or whichever—436? If you'd broken into the actual locker; by that time Monado #2 had been readmitted to hospital for therapy anyway; it wasn't like—I mean, the entire experiment— I figured if you had broken in, if you had found something out, we could have the discussion we're having now."

"So. You just bring people into the world, don't tell them they're clones, and then just run experiments on them?"

"No, we integrate—"

"But you don't tell them they're clones?"

"We do, when they're ready, sometimes it can be a bit of an… abrupt—"

"Yeah that sounds absolutely horrible! What a shit thing to spring on somebody!"

"Norm—Norman you're misunderstanding the purpose of these experiments,"

"Am I a clone? You gonna spring that on me next?"

"No. Of course not Norman."

"Jeez."

"They're not 'clones,' the way you seem to be using the term. They have just as much a claim to their own identities as their donor has. They just never physically lived through the memories they have. That doesn't make them any less of the person they are now than their original donor; everyone only exists in the present. Now, let's get past this. What about this folder, these clones—Monado #2—what has this all got to do with Patterson? Why did you come here?"

"Ah. Well, I was—trying to follow up on the disappearance of Wilhelm Monado; it seemed—suspicious, to say the least, very sudden,"

"Right, and I'm trying to explain that the disappearance of Will Monado has more to do with this recurring breach in confidentiality agreements than you may realize; I'm not even quite sure he's involved in any drug schemes at all."

"No, I don't think he is." That's what had struck Norman as off about his being dragged to a rehab unit in the first place.

"Then—why are you researching his disappearance?"

"Um. So. I mean—I may have—I mean, if he's a clone, then everything's explained; he's been kidnapped by his evil look-alike,"

"No, he's been readmitted for clinical evaluation, to find out why—" if Sanis had been holding a pencil she would have snapped it in half— "he's trying to breach confidentiality and harm his nephews; we've just brought him in for routine talk therapy to help calm him down. It's a standard procedure to help with schizophrenic personality disorder."

"He's schizophrenic? The Monados?"

"Just—mild paranoia and hallucinations; it's what brought Monado #1's—attention to wanting to aid psychiatric treatment in the first place." Using numbers instead of names was growing frustrating. "Are the clones the only lead you have?"

That was a pretty big lead!

Not concerning Patterson, of course. Norman had to think fast.

"Ah, yeah, it's just—something doesn't add up. Rene was the one who got in a fight, not Robert, and yet the—"

"Yeah, well, Robert really did get in a fight too; it happens,"

"Over a ticket?"

"Yeah. Over the ticket I just told you about. Same mental health problems. Same exact set up. Only thing that differed was the patients they were in with, and since we managed to book Rene in the same mental health facilities even most of his fellow inmates were still pretty much the same,"

"So, the whole thing was a set up?"

"Ah well, not—necessarily; I mean, part of the very nature of the treatment is a bit of a set up if you like—"

"But both times Monado #2 sent the ticket, he wasn't supposed to have done so? So, he was trying to get out to the world the fact that cloning was occurring at Freemont's?"

"Does this have anything to do with trailing Patterson at all? Have you been doing anything you claim to be doing?"

"Yes, no I just—look Frances Hayworth, my friend, said she specifically didn't want a clone; she's scared of them, and yet, downstairs, there's a form all filled out, ready and waiting to get her to sign—to consent to cloning. Now why would they do that? I saw that! That's not something I just hypothesized."

"Frances—"

The manager from Freemont knew Frances' case. "Yeah no Frances did say originally she wanted a twin; they just— didn't get along well, so we had to get rid of the twin,"

"You what?"

116

"We got rid of the twin; she's living in Miami now, I think, pretty happy with the situation, uh, we have this policy," the manager was explaining to Sanis as well now, "where if we have something a bit delicate to discuss with one of the patients we bring in Hugh Cossimer? It's kinda you know, a good trade off; he's great at getting people comfortable, relaxing them down to understanding everything's gonna be fine. Anyway, he was actually gonna talk to Frances today about a standard release form abnegating any strange legal problems now her twin's technically been released from the program; maybe, you saw--"

"The—you just let her clone go? She has schizophrenia!"

"Ah no, so, actually that was part of the problem, I think, personally, as to why they didn't get along so well; her twin was pretty well-adapted mentally, apparently, ah—she's actually agreed to undergo a few clinical trials to try to figure out why—"

"Ok. Ok. What about the signatures? The signatures on a lot of the other cloning contracts were all shaky—like they'd been drugged—!"

"Yeah, a lot of the medications used to deal with schizoaffective disorders cause tremors, Norman. Remember, this is specialized therapy; the donors are usually all suffering some sort of severe mental illness."

"Ok. Why would Robert eat the luggage ticket I showed him?"

"Severe. Mental. Illness."

Opportunities for discovering more information were growing slim, "just one more—ok— just—why did Monado #2 just take out the intake forms? Why didn't he take out the entire contract that says 'I agree to be cloned' so Rene could read that? I mean that seems like far more damning evidence if he was actually trying to get out to the world the fact there's cloning, but, these," Norman pointed, "were the folders I found in the locker. These other folders were still in the safe, and these are the ones pertaining to Espinose being cloned; I would've thought he'd use the document that says, 'I'll be cloned,' if what you're saying is true—"

"Ah, well the hospital has to reference those clone release forms every time we handle Robert's treatment and since he's staying at the hospital—"

"In rehab—?"

"Yeah."

Ok, that wasn't a clue then.

"…I suppose Monado #2 just assumed it was too much of a risk we'd find out the actual contract was missing, but he hoped—you know, half of the proof a duplicate exists would be enough to go on."

"Right…."

"…So, were you going somewhere with that?"

"Um. So. You're saying Monado #2 tried to tell Rene he's a clone, before Rene found out he was a clone?"

"Well, we honestly don't know what Monado #2's trying to get out of this situation; that's why we've brought him in for therapy with his brother; try to understand what's going on,"

"So—you know, Rene says he's always known he was a clone,"

"Oh. Really?"

"Yeah. He says he's always known."

"Huh."

Again, this wasn't quite Sanis' jurisdiction.

If she'd been any more central to the program, she would have been furious to know Norman had actually seen Rene recently. The entire ploy behind moving Rene from Servways to Freemont almost instantaneously after his hearing had been an attempt to get him away from the volunteer he'd gotten a little too friendly with, splashing around secrets—like that damned ticket Wilhelm kept so insistently foiling secrecy with.

As it was, now Norman was still desperately trying to <u>find some way to</u> excuse himself.

"So why would Rene always know he was a clone, if—as you say, you wipe their memories,"

"Ah, well we don't *wipe* they're memories, right? Actually, it's—I'm quite jealous really, all that study, in the blink of an eye; get your PhD soon as you—"

"But you don't tell them they're clones. Rene knew he was a clone,"

"Ah, when did he—tell you that?"

"Just a few minutes ago,"

"Oh. Yes, well he's been going through isolationed quiet therapy for about four days now with Robert—"

"Yeah but he said he knew before that,"

"Then, I guess—they must've—not wiped his memories early enough; or, maybe, they began to form earlier in the cloning process than we previously thought?" That was an interesting hypothesis. Sanis didn't really know the science behind it, but she could bring it up with Gottfried sometime. "Alright. So… is that all you've got?"

"For now… yes."

CHAPTER 22

"So, you assaulted an orderly because you thought you were getting close to discovering an opiate-running scheme you now have absolutely no leads on?"

"No, I—defended myself against an orderly because I was trying to trace the movements of my friend, Frances; she's been taken against her will; she's frightened; she thinks they'll clone her without her consent,"

"Okay, well, for one thing, we would never clone anyone without their consent; it simply costs too much, alright?"

"Well, she's disappeared now, with the same person I last saw Rene alive with—"

"I thought you said you just saw Rene?"

"They told me he was dead at Servways! And Freemont!"

"Yeah, well, I don't know what—that was some burcaucratic nightmare you can take that complaint up with the board of directors; Norman, does this even have anything to do with Patterson?"

"No! It has to do with a cloning operation!"

"Ok. Alright." So, there was a reason they'd retired him early. "I'm gonna go now; I've just wasted an hour."

"What? So, you're not gonna do anything about this? You have to help me find my friend! Frances—she—"

"Oh God, okay. Look. Can you just look up—whose—what's your friend's name again?"

"Frances Hayworth,"

"Oh yeah, Frances actually just got sent back early," one of the orderlies had had to accompany her, "she tried to pour a soda all over Hugh Cossimer for some reason,"

"Oh." For some reason, this gave Norman a sinking feeling.

119

"So, she's in her residential ward now?"

"Yeah,"

"Would you like to call her up?" Sanis was trying to be ameliorating.

"No, it's alright,"

"Okay,"

"So, what should we do about the—" the orderly's manager turned to Sanis now. "Can we go ahead and process him?"

"Yeah, I guess so, there's nothing to mitigate circumstances,"

"What?" Norman was instantly far more alert than he had been even discovering clones.

"Alright, sir, if you'd like to step out into the hallway now,"

"No wait—Sanis—you can't just let them charge me!"

"Norman, feel blessed you're not being charged with wasting police time," That was what, 3 search warrants he'd weaseled out of headquarters? For no reason?

"What? No, look, I'm sorry—I was told my friend had—" the county police returned to collect Norman's lock picking kit and put it in an evidence bag.

"Alright, sir, we're charging you with aggravated assault—"

"No this is insane; look—the orderly—where's the orderly I hit over the head? Can I just see him?"

"No sir, you cannot!" the manager had taken over now.

"I just wanna apologize—no! He's the one who presses charges! I want to explain my situation to him! —Look, I've got a flawless record; you can check this sort of incident is not—characteristic; I was under the impression a mass conspiracy was cloning mental patients against their will; I thought I would be exterminated as a witness—"

"Yes, well, you do need to know, sir: that confidentiality agreement you signed holds up under oath in court, as well."

"What?" Oh great. No one was going to back him up? He'd be charged with delusions!

"Ugh. Norman, please try to understand this is why bureaucratic procedurals are in place. I would've stopped you, if I'd known—"

"Are you gonna let them put me away? You're gonna let them put me away!"

"You assaulted an orderly!"

"I thought—….."

Last time he ever listened to a mad woman and believed she had all the facts in place. "I need a lawyer! I need a lawyer!"

"You'll be provided with a public defendant in due course—"

Someone rapped on the glass. It was the orderly Norman'd concussed.

"Hey, yeah I'm here with my lawyer; I'd like to discuss a settlement out of court with Mr. Cromel, and see about dropping charges,"

Wade had put in a good word for Norman.

Word spread like wildfire, the moment it was made clear that this assault on an orderly hadn't been instigated by a patient, but a volunteer still wearing his badge for the visitor volunteer program.

Wade was friends with the orderly Norman had concussed. Soon as the name 'Norman Cromel' was mentioned in association with the incident, he'd called Victor—the concussed orderly—for further details. He'd been worried Norman was losing his mind.

"Look, he's a nice chap; I think he might be fading a bit round the edges; he had a real bad blow recently, one of his patient volunteers killed himself; I think he's just—you know, not used to not being able to do anything about—you know, a sudden death." He'd calmed Victor into almost feeling bad for Norman.

Fred Bently, the guard between the gates at Servways, had vouched for Norman too.

Victor's lawyer proved decent enough.

"Look, you're retired, you served your community a long time; I understand that. You think someone's in trouble, you come rushing to their aid. It's just, you've gotta understand, that, from my client's point of view, it wasn't aid he received. It was a blow to the head."

"I'm so—I'm so sorry about that. I really am. I told you—I just—"

"Yeah, well, we're not here to press charges, we just, want to discuss the options for an out of court settlement; does that sound like a fair option? Do you agree?"

"Yes, yes that would be very appreciated. Thank you,"

At first, Norman briefly entertained suspicions this change in plans regarding his arrest could only be motivated by some secret evil plan, but he couldn't figure out what that might be.

Then, as the orderly's requested remunerations became apparent, Norman began to feel more and more as though he might be the evil one here.

Victor only asked for Norman to pay for medical expenses to cover the cost of doctoring the concussion, and to cover paid leave for three days while his head healed, because his employer's insurance didn't pay for that.

"Of course, of course."

"I also think, and this is just me, personally, speaking," the lawyer coughed slightly, "that a few extra euros, to offset psychological distress, might be in order,"

"Yes, yes of course."

CHAPTER 23

The next four days were very difficult for Norman. He steered clear of volunteering to talk with Servways' patients— didn't even pick up the phone for a while. He didn't know how he'd be able to face the orderlies back at Servways. Victor had mentioned their input. He felt so ashamed.

All his notes on the Rene case, as it had been unofficially filed in his mind, were left in a stack, untouched, at the side of his kitchen counter. Three days in, he noticed the print-out of digitally scanned microfilm he had originally photocopied while researching Rene's family tree was doctored around the edges, with just a faint rebrushing, to add 'Wilhelm Monado' beside his brother 'Gottfried'. Of course. Even the old pre-digital copies would have been doctored. Sanis had said the program had been active since 2016. It was, at least, proof positive Wilhelm was the clone and Gottfried had been cloned; for what good that could do— provide some closure….

Honestly, it all added up.

The only hitch had been that suicide alert from Wade; without it, Norman would never have gone investigating at Freemont. He would have simply assumed Rene transferred, without bothering to tell him where he went, because they were, after all, only acquaintances, and that would have been the end of it. No follow up.

Three weeks later, he finally accepted a request to visit Vincent, another patient at Servways. He only remembered, when he was climbing out of his car in the parkng lot, that he had entirely forgotten his last scheduled appointment with Vincent. It had been scheduled to occur the same day hc'd broken into Freemont's Cloning basements.

122

Chagrined, he put himself through the pain of greeting Bently as though nothing had changed. He was just entering the visitor's entrance when Hugh Cossimer arrived, with his habitual miniature retinue of two or three reporters. Their routines must have been similar.

"Yes, yes, no no. Just a short visit today," he was saying.

So, Hugh really did just visit lonely old men and women like Frances, to give them the thrill of chatting with a celebrity.

Norman watched him walk away down another brick path towards a visitor's center that led to another section of the Protective Facility's ward-system.

Even Wade hadn't been told fully about the cloning aspect of Norman's assault on Victor. As far as he knew, Victor had just mistaken Norman for a patient.

"So glad you got out of that okay,"

"Yes, thank you—thank you, so much for putting in a good word."

A successful conversation with Vincent prompted Norman to feel confident enough he could ask:

"Did they ever sort out those claims Rene was dead?"

"Uh—what?"

O-oh. Rene alive and well must have been one of the tidbits of information the confidentiality contract was meant to restrain.

Or maybe Wade had been instructed not to let Norman near Rene, if it could be helped, after he'd told Rene not to testify about his delusions at the Collins hearing.

"Was that—are you not allowed to talk about that?"

"Oh no, no, I—thought Rene was dead. Pretty sure…." *Was Norman doing okay?*

"It was in the system then? That he's deceased? That's where you saw—? When they told you?"

"Ah, no, I actually got a phone call from one of the retired board of directors; he let me know personally, was I think, uh, a member of the family—"

"Gottfried Monado?"

"Yeah, that's right,"

"You're sure it was him?"

"Well it came from his phone number; still keyed in special, you know, special —um— touch dial activated security sort of thing, for the—to keep the patients off it."

"Was it—the person who spoke—did they have, kind of a cockney accent? Real pronounced? Said day like 'die'?"

"Yeah, that's right,"

So, it had been Wilhelm on the phone, not Gottfried. Norman would bet anything. Wilhelm had started Norman's entire wild goose chase. Same fingerprints, so he could use the security pad on Gottfried's interhospital line.

Then, Gottfried must have found out, and felt forced to play along—now outsiders like Wade believed his nephew deceased. The funeral arrangements, the service—wouldn't want anyone knowing an identical set of fingerprints could be used to operate his touch dial, eh? Clever bastard, mocking up an obituary just in case—and just in time—before grieving friends rolled round. Even the doctor at Freemont….

Just let it go, Norman told himself, driving home. Keep out of trouble. It would be insane not to. There was no conspiracy. He simply had a sense he'd glimpsed something evil, some nefariousness bureaucracy managed to shrug off with pat explanations. But there was so very little Norman could do. In reality, all the heroics of protagonism boiled down to a stubborn sort of madness—the sort of eccentric who refused, to an unhealthy degree, to live in the world as it was.

Two days later he received a text from Freemont, asking if he would like to visit Frances; she was requesting him as a conversation partner.

'Sorry,' he finally decided to text back, 'I won't be available at that time.' He left it at that; it was for the best. He closed his phone.

Time to return to normalcy. Try something new; get more paprika to go with his eggplant recipe. Let calm twenty-somethings wade through the mess of others' delusions. He simply got caught up in them. Or couldn't see that a clone ought to be called a twin and an original a donor because he was too bored to admit reality didn't have vast evils that were so easily identifiable.

All he had found was one ornery clone who felt like he was stuck in a system he wanted to tell the world about— and wasn't allowed to. Trapped where he didn't want to stay. And even then, his torture turned out to be nothing but talk therapy. Just an old has-been of an idiot trying to see the importance in his own littleness, trying to make a mark; to break free, get the word out; trying for a truth he'd never—

Norman picked up his phone again.

He called Demetry.

"Hey. I think I have another job for you. It's a bit more complex,"

"You've been listening to crazies again?"

"Yeah, I figured I could use your steadying influence," just in case he was going mad. Demetry was sure to come in useful putting a stop to that. He had, after all, pulled himself away from a pyramid scheme.

"Alright. If you accompany again."

"Yeah, yeah, I'll be there to help,"

"What is it?"

"Well, have you ever broken someone out of a psychiatric unit before?"

The least Norman could do would be to get an old man out of dreaded 'talk therapy' with a brother he disliked. Let Wilhelm tell a stranger his side of the story instead. Let him have an audience, even just an audience of one, before they whisked him away again.

ABOUT THE AUTHOR

E. L. Murray is a shady conglomeration of several authors and a grandmother. Between us we have a degree in Assyriology from Cambridge, back pain, and a dog. Please visit slugandbubblebooks.com for more information and news about upcoming publications.

www.ingramcontent.com/pod-product-compliance
Lightning Source LLC
Chambersburg PA
CBHW060439130626
46555CB00005B/2420